GW00801627

Cariad Lloyd

THE CHRISTMAS WISH-TASTROPHE

HODDER

Illustrated by Ma Pe

HODDER CHILDREN'S BOOKS

First published in Great Britain in 2024 by Hodder & Stoughton

1 3 5 7 9 10 8 6 4 2

A CIP catalogue record for this book
is available from the British Library.

Hardback ISBN 978 1 444 97148 4
Paperback ISBN 978 1 444 97149 1

Printed and bound in Great Britain by
Clays Ltd, Elcograf, S.p.a.

The paper and board used in this book
are made from wood from responsible sources.

Hodder Children's Books
An imprint of
Hachette Children's Group
Part of Hodder & Stoughton Limited
Carmelite House
50 Victoria Embankment
London EC4Y 0DZ

The authorised representative in the EEA is Hachette Ireland, 8 Castlecourt Centre, Castleknock Road, Castleknock, Dublin 15, D15 YF6A, Ireland

An Hachette UK Company
www.hachette.co.uk

www.hachettechildrens.co.uk

For my loves, B and W.

'For what do we live, but to make sport for our neighbours, and laugh at them in our turn?'

Jane Austen, *Pride and Prejudice*

Chapter One TROUBLE

Lydia Marmalade was a very clever girl. She didn't know it yet, but she was. She did know that she liked to daydream, sing loudly to herself … *and* she **believed** in wishes. She knew sometimes they came true, if you wished really, *really* as hard as you possibly could.

But right now, Lydia's heart was heavy and she had stopped believing in wishes. She had too many other things to worry about.

So far in her life, she had managed to stay out of trouble, big trouble. Of course, she had been in lots of *little* trouble, like most interesting people – **scrapes**, **japes** and **hullabaloos**, but no Big T Trouble.

Now she was in a trouble she couldn't get out of.

Lydia wriggled in her seat, watching the empty fields pass by and snuggling into her many shawls to keep warm, but her feet were still **freezing**. Oh, you may think you've been cold before, but you haven't. Yes, you've seen snow, or you've been outside without your coat, but you have never been as cold as Lydia Marmalade was then. Because Lydia lived in olden times.

Lydia didn't know she was living in *olden times*; she thought she was just living in *times*. But she was, in fact, living in **1812**. So there was no heating you could turn on and she wasn't even in a car, she was in a carriage, pulled by horses (because it was 1812).

Lydia had no fridge, no scooter, no bedside lamps, no television or even … **internet**. But before you put the book down in shock and need a strong cup of tea to revive you, you must remember that if you have never had these things, you don't miss them.

Lydia knew how to miss things though. That's not something only modern nowadays people feel. Lydia was **missing** something very greatly – her home. Her bedroom, her creaky stairs, her two chickens that had survived the local fox's many attempts to eat them – and, most of all, her mum.

Lydia's mother had died, just two months ago. So, with every mile she travelled **further** away from home, it felt like she was losing her mum all over again.

Her father had died when she was small and Lydia couldn't really remember him, so she didn't miss him exactly – but she missed the idea of a dad, having someone who puts you on their shoulders or tickles you till you scream. She couldn't recall his face or voice, and now she was worried one day she would feel the same about her mum. She didn't have a photo of them (in case you forgot the olden times bit) but she could remember being hugged a lot and laughing. The laughter sounded as if it was coming from down a long corridor, and if she listened hard, she could still catch the echo of it.

She wasn't sure how long she had been riding in the bumpy carriage, but it was long enough for her bottom to have gone numb. As dusk fell, she began to wonder if she'd make it to her new home before nightfall.

She **wriggled** again (Lydia was a great wriggler) and a small bundle on her lap gave a little yip. It was Colin, her dog. He yipped again, poking his nose out of the many layers of blankets she had tried to hide him in, sniffing the new air.

'Colin!' she hissed, 'Get back in!' Colin gave a snort through his nose to show he thoroughly disapproved of being ordered around, before reluctantly snuggling back into his layered nest.

'Everything all right down there, miss?' the coach driver called to her.

'Oh yes! Very good, thanks!' said Lydia in what she hoped was a jolly tone.

Colin was Lydia's best friend in the whole world. Colin was a sausage dog, but Colin didn't know that so it was best never to refer to him as such. Colin was simply a Colin. Lydia had found him when he was a pup, stuck in a bed of reeds by the pond in her village, and her mother had named him. She had thought he was trying to escape the water, but as she rescued him she realised he had been trying to get in. Even now, if he saw a pond or lake, his favourite thing in the world was to jump straight in. But his **bestest** thing to do was to curl up to Lydia at night, like a hot little bean.

Lydia had been given strict instructions not to bring Colin with her to her new house. And yet, here he was, on her lap. This was how Lydia often got into trouble – she didn't mean to break rules, but if she disagreed with the rule, she was sure she could show the person how wrong it was, and then they'd agree with her and change the rule. (This wasn't always successful ...)

The wind began to howl, and the bare trees swayed, spiky branches grasping at each other. A robin flew out of a tree and past the carriage. Something caught

Lydia's eye on the branch the bird had flown from. The branch itself seemed to be **shimmering**, reflecting a light that wasn't there. She blinked again and it was gone. A small red squirrel scampered down and stopped to pile acorns into a hole in the tree.

Lydia remembered her mum talking about the **magic** you could find in a forest, the creatures that lived amongst the branches and leaves, and hid from the real world. Her mind drifted back to looking for wood sprites with her mum last winter, but she pushed the memory away.

Lydia longed to arrive, yet was afraid of what she would find when they did. She reached into her reticule (that's what they called your handbag in ye olden times) and found some biscuits she had been saving. She broke one in half and Colin's black, wet nose reappeared from between the blankets, sniffing to find the delicious treat, and then he quickly **gobbled** it up.

She was so tired, her head started to bob as the cold night drew in around them. She couldn't remember how long they had been riding for by now, but she knew she was moving far away, far away from the people she had known and who had known her mother. There was Annie who ran the wool shop, who Colin loved almost as much as Lydia, and Fred the baker, who always told her when the buns would be done so she could be first in line to get a warm one. Her friends. Beech Cottage, her home.

Suddenly the carriage **lurched** as it hit a hole in the dirt road. Lydia sat upright again and, as they rounded a bend, a house came into view. **Peppomberley**, her new home.

Peppomberley was not a normal house. It was *huge*. If you imagine a big house in the now times, then imagine **FOUR** of those houses next to each other. And then another four on top, that's Peppomberley. No wait, add another one on top of them all. That's it. Now you've imagined a **MASSIVE** house. That's Peppomberley.

Peppomberley looked like the sort of house your parents might drag you to on a weekend, pretending to enjoy looking at old rooms but really wanting to go to the gift shop and the cafe. But in 1812 Peppomberley wasn't a house for buying key rings and fancy shortbread, it was a real house in which real people lived. The Partridges, Lydia's new family.

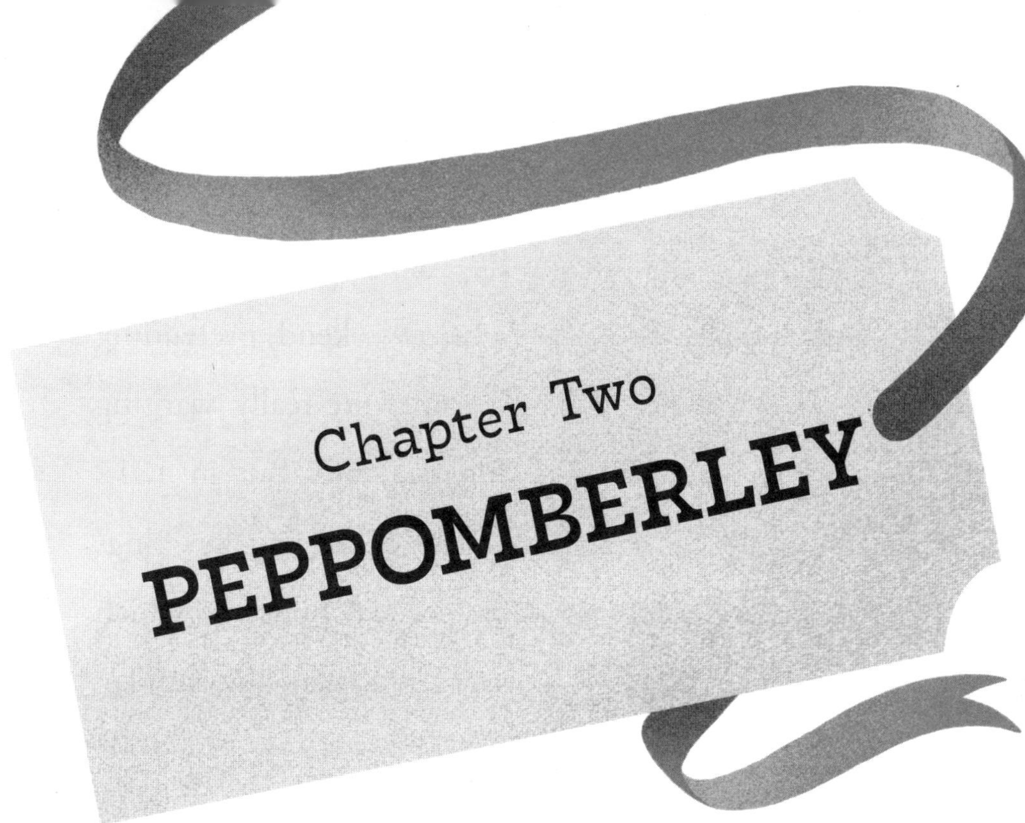

Chapter Two
PEPPOMBERLEY

Lydia stared at the house as they rode closer, eyes widening. It really was enormous; she couldn't imagine how many bedrooms it had. Her home in Hopperton had been a farmhouse with two bedrooms that her grandfather had lived in when he was a boy. How would she find her way round Peppomberley? She stared at the many sparkling windows and tried to imagine her own home directly in front of it, comparing how much Beech Cottage would be dwarfed by Peppomberley.

What if she got lost forever? Would they give her a map?

***

It had been early September when Lydia had first heard Lady Partridge's name. Her mum had been getting weaker by the day and while Lydia had insisted she would be fine to live by herself with Colin, in her heart she knew it wouldn't be possible.

So, Lydia's mum wrote to a rich family she'd known a long time ago, who Lydia had never heard of, her hand shaky but her writing as beautiful as ever – and that was the first time Lydia saw the strange word on the envelope:

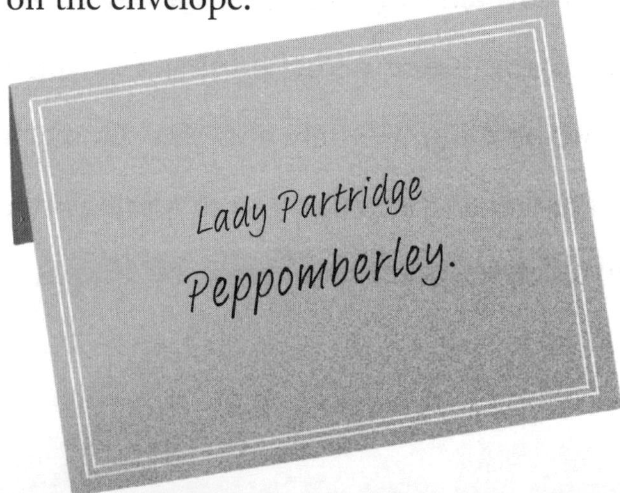

Lydia's mum hadn't told her much at all about Lady Partridge. And then it had been too late to ask.

Lady Partridge's opulent carriage had arrived in Hopperton in October. Children from the village came running after it as it headed towards Lydia's house, chasing and shouting at the pale grey horses pulling it, like a **fairytale queen** had come to town. Lydia was still in Beech Cottage then, with the neighbours who had loved her mother fussing and helping.

Lydia watched from the window as Lady Partridge stepped out of the carriage straight into the dirt outside the house, **wrinkling** her nose at the mud. She looked older than her mother, but also fresher, her hands covered in beautiful black lace gloves. She swept into the house without knocking and Colin began to **bark** immediately.

Lady Partridge kicked her foot in Colin's direction. **'Take that outside, child!'**

Lydia was so shocked she did as she was told, even though she had never in her life put Colin outside. She gave him a whispered sorry and gently pushed him out into the garden.

'Let me look at you then.' Lady Partridge took Lydia in from the top of her frizzy brown hair to her scuffed shoes. 'I am sorry about your mother, Catherine—' She paused and appraised the room: the blackened fireplace, the piles of books, the mess. 'I am sorry to hear of her passing.' She stepped around the word *dead*, but Lydia still heard it in her head. 'She wrote to me some time ago and informed me she required a home for her daughter, Lydia Marmalade—'

'Yes! It was in September …' Lydia interrupted. Lady Partridge stared at her. 'I beg your pardon,' Lydia whispered.

'She informed me you were a good and modest child who listens well and can sing brightly.'

Lydia blinked. Who was her mother talking about? Lydia the chatterbox? Lydia who would chase the birds away when she shout-screamed any song she had tried to learn? Lydia stared at this burglar of her life, wondering what advice her mother would give her. She didn't need to think twice; she could still see her in her chair by the big window. Knitting in hand, smiling at Lydia. 'Be honest, Lydia – but not so honest you scare everyone.'

Lydia **shuffled** her feet. *Be honest, Lydia.* She had promised her mum she would try her hardest to fit in at Peppomberley and make something of her life.

'Yes, Lady Partridge, I *try* to be very good.'

'Excellent. And you have had some lessons? You know French?'

'I know my letters and my numbers in English. I know some French.' Lydia knew a song in French about a dog that **farted** so much it exploded.

'Your mother was exquisite at French!'

Was she? Lydia thought. That was news to her. 'Did you know my mother well, Lady Partridge?' she asked.

'What? No! A distant relative!' Lady Partridge declared. She stared down at Lydia, making no attempt to hide her disappointment.

Lydia remembered the **warmth** and **love** she would feel when her mum looked at her, and she felt her eyes fill up. She swallowed hard, instinctively knowing Lady Partridge would not tolerate tears.

Lady Partridge let out a **sigh** and muttered to herself.

'The state of the house and the child! Well, it is settled, although there will be much work to do to make you a *proper* lady. I shall send the carriage for you on the sixth of December. Then you will join me at Peppomberley.'

Lydia wanted to scream *no*, but she just nodded and looked at the floor.

'We shall sell this,' Lady Partridge gestured vaguely at her home, '*cottage* to pay for your food and board. Your mother left little in the way of support for you, which was most clumsy of her. It shan't fetch much, of course.'

Lady Partridge headed for the door, putting on a large bonnet festooned with peacock feathers. Lydia exhaled as quietly as she could, thinking it was over, then suddenly the feathers swung back around to face her—

'Understand this, Lydia Marmalade. If you are not good, modest, quiet and everything I expect of a girl of your age, you shall be removed from my house. Where you live after that will be no concern of mine. A workhouse for poor children, no doubt.'

Lydia found herself nodding. A workhouse? She had never seen one, but she knew it was where you were sent when you had no money and no family to help you. A terrifying cellar **full of spiders**, with the door locked, flashed in her mind.

Lady Partridge hesitated and picked up Lydia's mother's shawl from her chair. It was a delicate cornflower blue. For a moment Lydia thought she saw her cheeks flush, then she straightened.

'I will give you until Christmas Day. If you can behave like a *proper* lady until then, you may become a member of my household, indeed my family. If not … I have made it clear what will become of you.' She placed the shawl carefully back on to the moth-eaten chair. 'Oh, and your dog is not welcome at Peppomberley. I tolerate no such useless animals. Be sure to be rid of him before the carriage calls for you.'

Lady Partridge did something with her face – Lydia realised that it was an attempt at a smile – and swooped out the door.

Lydia **slumped** on to the chair. For a second it felt as if nothing had happened, and her life was the same. She looked around the **dishevelled** cottage, and heard its silence. Then she knew it *had* changed. Everything had.

Colin ran in and curled on to her lap, licking her nose and letting out a **whimper**.

'I know, Col.' Lydia rubbed his head. 'Maybe it'll be all right in the morning.'

Lydia used her best voice, like her mum had always done for her when she had to do something she didn't want to, but she knew she wasn't convincing either of them.

***

As the carriage finally drew into Peppomberley's stables, Lydia clutched Colin's warm body close. Her home sold, all her possessions tied to the top of the carriage, her mother's shawl around her shoulders.

She tried to focus on holding Colin still, but something was distracting her. How had her mother known Lady Partridge? How did Lady Partridge know her mother could speak French, when she was just a distant relative? Lydia's brain started to **whirr**, heading towards a thousand possibilities, as it did whenever something confused her – what if? But how? Why? She took a deep breath. This was a mystery indeed, and one she would hopefully have enough time to solve.

Lydia pulled her shawl tight as she headed towards the **grand house**, and resolved not to let the mystery go.

Chapter Three
MEETINGS

Lydia had hoped she would be shown to her room immediately so she could **hide** Colin, who was still wrapped in blankets in her arms. As she stepped out of the carriage a young maid (probably only a few years older than Lydia) was coming towards her, and before Lydia knew it a small pair of hands **reached** for the Colin-bundle.

'I'll take that for you, miss.'

'No!' Lydia exclaimed so loudly the girl took a step back.

The maid – confused – reached out to grab the Colin-bundle again, but Lydia held on. She was quite short for her age, but her arms were surprisingly strong. She spent a lot of time climbing trees and hanging from the branches, so she was oddly hard to take things off. The maid stepped back and stared. (Lydia was fairly used to not always doing what was to be expected of a young girl in 1812.)

The tug o'war had made Colin wriggle inside his bundle. **'Not now, Col!'** Lydia whispered into the blankets.

'Are you talking to those blankets?' the maid asked.

Lydia didn't mean to lie, but as you may know, this is how many a lie can begin. Bringing Colin with her meant Lydia was going to have to tell lots of little lies. She was **breaking a rule**, and the key to breaking rules is to do it boldly.

'Yes, I did just talk to my blankets,' Lydia said. 'It's what we do in Hopperton, we talk to blankets to make sure they don't get lonely.' Lydia bent her head. 'Great job of keeping me warm all this way!' Colin wiggled again, but Lydia wrestled him still. Those strong arms were now coming in useful.

The maid looked at her, a little worried now. 'You best go in; Lady Partridge wants to see you.'

'Thank you!' Lydia chimed cheerily, hiding her fear.

As she walked towards the house, she could hear the maid's voice as she muttered to herself. 'Not like Lady Partridge's usual guests. She don't look like a proper lady! Or act like one neither.'

Lydia headed to the stone stairs and trudged towards the huge, black front door, the harsh wind stinging her cheeks. She steadied herself and looked at the view from the **grand entrance**. It was beautiful. Even as the grounds gave over to winter, she could imagine how wonderful they would be once flowers surrounded the lake, and the woods teemed with birds in the spring. But would she still be here by then? Or would winter be how she always remembered Peppomberley?

The door opened and Lydia stepped inside, **gasping out loud**. It was as if she was in a doll's house, not a real home. There was a chandelier, drapes, she could even see a piano in another room! Everything was so incredibly grand.

She was staring at the thick rug underneath her worn-out boots when a man in a long black coat appeared from behind the door. His back was straight like a plant that had been tied to canes. **'Follow me,'** he said. His voice was low and raspy, like he needed a cough, and he strode off down the corridor.

Lydia followed his large steps, still clutching Colin. The man showed her into the drawing room, its windows looking directly out on to Peppomberley's lake. The walls were painted a pale turquoise, and thick teal curtains swished down to the floor.

Lydia couldn't help thinking that the entire

downstairs of Beech Cottage would fit in this one room.

'Is something wrong, child?' Lady Partridge's shrill voice punctured her thoughts and Lydia **jumped** out of her skin.

Lady Partridge was sitting at an ornate wooden desk. She **wrinkled** her nose, just as she had done in Hopperton. **'I trust the journey was fair.'**

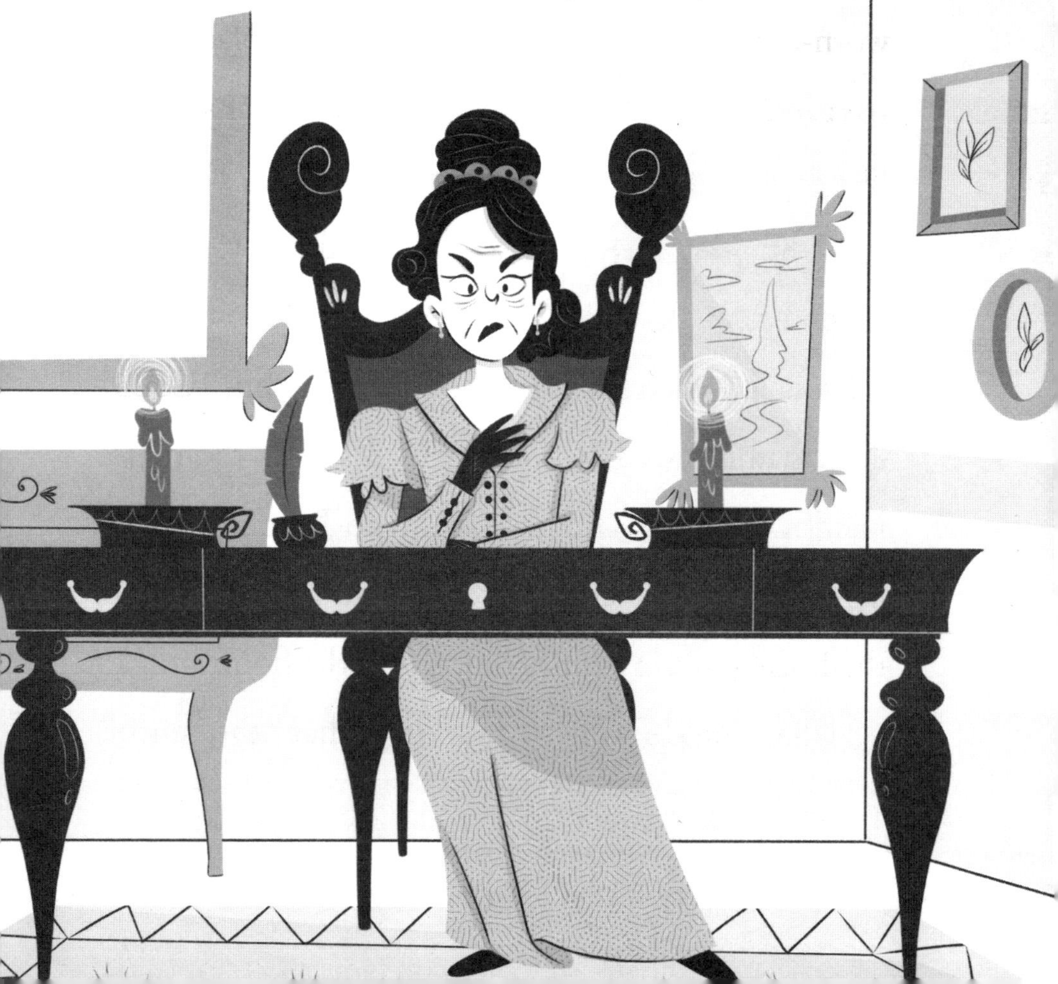

Lydia went to open her mouth and then realised Lady Partridge did not expect her to answer.

'I also trust you found a new home for your dog?'

Lydia froze. But it was clear Lady Partridge now *wanted* an answer.

'Er, yes, I did find a … place he will be living.' *Not an outright lie*, thought Lydia.

'Very good. Your lessons won't begin until after the winter season, after you have passed your trial and proved yourself a *proper* young lady.' She paused and gave Lydia a cold look. 'Starting with dinner tonight. You will speak only when spoken to and cause *no trouble at all.* Do you understand?'

'Yes, of course, Lady Partridge!' Lydia blurted out. She gave her best curtsey, or what she hoped was one, having never curtseyed before.

Lady Partridge frowned. 'Ronalds!' she called in a pitch that made Colin twitch again. The man in the black coat reappeared. 'Please take Miss Marmalade to her room to change before dinner.' She eyed Lydia's shabby travelling clothes.

'Very well, ma'am.'

Ronalds **marched** up the staircase. He led Lydia down another long corridor, with doors either side, each one closed. It felt as if half the house was shut up – there were dust sheets over furniture, and abandoned packing boxes exploding with bits of straw.

Lydia tried to remember which way they had come so she could find her way out again, but everything was blurring into one long corridor that had no end. Ronalds turned again, up more stairs, mumbling to himself. Occasionally they would pass another servant who would dart out of the way and try to hide their whole body against the wall. 'Windows, Gregory!' Ronalds would snarl, or, 'Aggie, the hearth!'

They climbed another set of small stairs, and Ronalds finally opened a little door that he had to stoop to look through.

'Here is your room, Miss Marmalade.'

Lydia stopped and stared. The room was modest but there was a round window with an opening halfway so you could tip a semi-circle of glass open. The bed looked comfy and a pretty water jug and bowl stood in front of a stand with a mirror. It looked almost ... homely.

Ronalds was glaring at Lydia, looking annoyed about something.

'Thank you, this is a lovely room,' she offered, forcing a tight smile.

Ronalds tutted, but didn't move. Finally he burst out, exasperated, 'You have to *excuse* me, girl!'

Lydia was **surprised** to remember that she was a member of the household and would have to learn how to act accordingly if she had any chance of passing Lady Partridge's high **'proper lady'** standards before Christmas Day.

'Oh, sorry! You're excused, I mean!'

'Very well, miss,' he said. As he closed the door, Lydia could hear him muttering to himself. 'Gone before Christmas, I'll wager five shillings on it.'

***

Lydia stared out of the window. The lake was on the right, surrounded by a forest of sleeping winter trees, and rolling hills in the distance. She could sense the wood sleeping, and although it lacked all the chaos of Hopperton with its chickens and its mud and its maypole at an angle, it had a peaceful beauty. The house's formal gardens were bordered by the woodland, and something about the **neatness** of the gardens next to the **wildness** of the trees reminded her of her mum – how serene she had looked sitting in their messy house doing her stitching. A steady calm in amongst the chaos.

Lydia sighed, wishing she could return to that place that would only ever exist now in her memory. She went to turn away, yet something caught her eye. It seemed like the branches of the trees were **sparkling**, **twinkling**, as she had seen from the carriage. 'They don't like to be seen,' her mum used to say. 'But sometimes they can't help but show off their wings.'

Lydia blinked again and it was gone. She turned away: she needed to be here, not in her head again.

She locked her bedroom door and, to be sure, pushed a chair against it too. Then she finally plopped down the bundle on the bed.

'It's safe now, Col.'

The blanket **trembled** until Colin appeared from under it, shaking himself from head to bottom to tail and back again. He gave Lydia a yip and then jumped up and licked her nose. She hugged him tight. 'Oh, Col,' she said, 'this is it, this is home now.' She gestured around the room. Colin gave another yip and then dropped his head on to his paws in acceptance. Lydia filled the wash bowl with water, which he gratefully lapped up.

Lydia carefully undid her mother's shawl and held it to her face, taking in the remains of her smell, before folding it carefully and placing it under her pillow. Then she walked to the washbowl stand and looked into the mirror above it. Her thick brown hair was the only part of her appearance that reminded her of her mother, although Lydia struggled to tame hers. She saw her bright blue eyes, so unlike her mum's brown eyes, yet they held the same shape. Perhaps life at Peppomberley would be quiet, dull and simple. If she could spend the winter season as she had today, she could sail through to Christmas Day, pass the test required to be a **proper lady** and then … what then? How could this ever feel like home?

Lydia sat next to Colin and stroked his velvet ears, playfully flopping them both back so he looked like he had a bow on his head. He shook them, gave her a look of Colin miffed-ness which meant 'geroff' and then placed his nose on her lap. She smiled. As long as they were together, everything would somehow be all right.

***

Lydia began to feel sleepy and could feel herself drifting off, her body still imagining the bumps of the carriage, when she heard voices outside her door.

She tiptoed towards the door, pushed back the chair she had wedged there earlier, and carefully opened it the fractioniest of a tiny fraction, to see who was coming.

'Ronalds! Keep up! You are not as old as you look.' A tall gentleman with thick black curly hair was marching down the corridor. Lydia thought it must be Edmund, Lady Partridge's son – her only pride and joy – who her mother had told her about. Lydia slid back into her room as much as she could whilst still listening.

'I want to see if Miss Marmalade has whiskers like a field mouse or feathers like a chicken, as the maids are claiming!'

'Lord Partridge, your mother has ordered the girl to recuperate before your guests arrive this evening.' That low voice was **unmistakeably** Ronalds. 'I expect you will not need long to see she is not one of your mother's *usual* acquaintances. She will find it hard to make herself at home in such a grand and fine house as Peppomberley.' Ronalds attempted a light-hearted laugh, but it sounded like he was having a coughing fit.

'Ah, you think she will not pass Mama's test then! Very well, I'll see her soon enough. I only wish I had been consulted on a ward entering the house. After all, now I am come of age it is I who am to be running the estate!' Edmund said.

'Indeed, of course, and I agree, sir.'

And then, thankfully, Lydia heard the footsteps retreat.

Lydia squeezed her eyes tight and dug her nails into her palms as she had done at her mother's funeral, when she hadn't wanted anyone to see how sad she was, and yet this time the tears sneaked out of her eyes. They were talking about her as if she wasn't a real person with feelings, as if her life was just a joke to them. Edmund was clearly as bad as Ronalds.

Lydia knew that Edmund had been the heir – and since his father's death a couple of years ago, he was the new Lord of Peppomberley. *Heir* is an olde word, which has nothing to do with hair. In fact, you pronounce it as if there is no h at all. It should really be spelled 'air' , but English is never so simple as that (don't let us start on how we say ghost, we don't have the time…).

Lydia could feel her **heart racing** and remembered a game her mother played with her when she was frightened. What could she feel beneath her fingertips? She stroked Colin's round belly. What could she see now? She stared at the grey sky. What could she hear? She listened for the call of the roosting birds. She felt her breathing slow down. *Today she was here, today she was here*.

Finally, she fell asleep.

Chapter Four
HUNGRY

A couple of hours later, Lydia awoke with a start, thinking she was back in **Hopperton**. She shook her head, replacing her old bedroom with this new strange one. Then she realised her face was being licked.

'Colin!' she picked him up and looked him in the eyes. 'What's wrong, Collydrop?'

He **whimpered**, and she instantly knew – he was hungry. She had given him all the food she had stashed with her from the cottage. There was nothing left. How on earth was she going to keep Colin here if she couldn't feed him – or worse, take him outside? He gave her a look which implied, yes, she was right, he also needed a wee.

Lydia dressed quickly and stared at herself in the small looking glass. She saw that she was going to break more rules. And that was that. She sighed, swaddled up Colin again and set off.

Slipping out, she followed the corridor in the direction she had come from earlier. Colin gave a **whine**, and she squeezed the bundle to tell him to hang on. She walked and walked, past painting after painting of grand people. Lydia admired their huge dresses but thought they all looked rather **grumpy**, and it reminded her of what her mother had always said: 'Happiness falls where it wants, no matter how fine your purse is.'

As she reached the end of the long corridor, she

noticed a small door that was so flush with the wall, it was almost invisible, but she could see the outside edge of it. She pulled it open and found a simple set of stone steps leading down in a spiral. She could smell she was on the right track for food. It was **undeniably** the world's greatest smell of all … cake. The sweet vanilla-rich smell of a sponge rising in an oven was climbing up the stairs towards her. Lydia's stomach **rumbled**, as did Colin's.

As Lydia reached the bottom of the staircase, she heard a pleasant voice begin to sing a song that she had heard when she was small. Lydia paused for a moment, enjoying the quiet calm of the enclosed staircase.

The west is always calling you
But you shall never know
That what the west is calling you for
Is a lesson takes time to show

Lydia felt Colin wriggle and carefully pushed open the door to the kitchen. It smelt scrumptious; she could hardly stop her mouth from drooling at the thought of all the deliciousness that awaited her there.

'Good gracious!' she whispered out loud, as she saw not one, not two, but at least *seven* cakes sat in tins on the counter. Colin's stomach took over and he **leapt** out of her arms towards the cook standing at the bench with her back to them.

'COLIN!' Lydia hissed, filled with alarm. But it was too late: the cook let out a yelp and dropped the last cake. Colin began to **devour** it as only a happy dog can.

'Oh my giddy aunt, where have you come from, mister?' The cook whooshed around and saw Lydia.

'I'm so sorry!' Lydia blurted out, panicking. 'Oh, please don't tell Lady Partridge! I can explain! He's my dog, my best friend – I couldn't leave him behind.

But he's so hungry and your cake smells so good and ...'

The cook glanced at Colin (who had now dragged off a chunk of sponge as big as his head), back to Lydia's **horrified** face, and then she began to laugh. She was hooting and slapping her thighs and wiping her eyes with her apron. 'Oh my, Miss Marmalade, you know how to make an entrance!' She laughed some more and began to pick up the cake tin. 'Well, that's woken me up for sure, I'm in a fair doze this morning. You can have that chunk, young man, but that's it!'

Lydia stared at her in utter shock. 'You don't mind that we, that Colin ... ?'

'Come now, my love, cake is cake and as you can see I've got plenty here. Colin, eh? Well, that's a gentleman's name if ever I heard one. My name's Harriet and you can come and see me any time you fancy a little nibble. There's always a tidbit to be found here!'

Colin let out a **yip** of delight as he continued to devour his stolen treat.

'I'm afraid when he's hungry he does not care a fig about anything other than his stomach,' explained Lydia.

'You must be hungry too, Miss Marmalade, after all your travelling, I told them to tell me when you arrived.' Harriet tutted.

Harriet bustled her way over to a pantry full of goodness. Lydia could smell **spices** and **herbs** and see dead birds: partridges and pheasants hanging from the celling next to huge bunches of leaves that were drying. Everything about the kitchen was a perfect chaos of food and pans and jars, and Harriet weaved her way around it all effortlessly.

'Now what about … oh yes, this'll do nicely!'

Harriet took out a plump tea cake, popped it on to the range for a minute to toast, before spreading it with a thick layer of golden butter and an equally large measure of bright red strawberry jam, and serving it to Lydia. She grabbed some cold cuts of meat and placed them on a plate for Colin, who had by now finished the cake and was anxiously hanging around her skirts, hoping for some more.

Before Harriet set his plate down, she whisked Colin up, opened the back door and plonked him outside. 'You know what you need to do, Master Colin, come back when it's done.' She turned to Lydia, 'No one will see him there, Miss Marmalade. Now eat up and drink up too.'

Lydia bit into the soft tea cake filled with **squidgy** raisins and tasted the **perfect** strawberry jam. It was like tasting summer and she dropped her shoulders, just a little, for the first time since arriving at Peppomberley.

Harriet opened the back door just as Colin had his paw raised to it and set down his feast of yesterday's pork chops.

'Thank you so much, that was the best tea cake I've ever had,' said Lydia.

'Oh well, there's fine words for you, you'll give me a big head if you're not careful.' Harriet laughed again. Lydia realised she was nearly always smiling at something.

'Why do you need so many cakes?' Lydia asked.

'Ooh, there's a big dinner tonight! And I am under instructions to make a feast that will be remembered to Michaelmas! An accomplished young lady is attending, a Miss Marianne Braun, with her mother, Lady Agatha Braun. The gossip is that Lady Partridge is keen to impress on them how suitable Master Edmund – I mean, Lord Partridge – is for a match.' She gave Lydia a big wink. 'So, I thought to myself, what is more lovely than a huge sponge cake – to remind everyone that happiness is easily sought!' She began to mix a huge bowl of flour that drifted up in a cloud as she spoke. 'Tonight is the start of the winter season, Miss Marmalade, you'll be at ball after party after dance before you know it! It's non-stop until Twelfth Night!'

Twelfth Night is the sixth of January, and in olden times it was another big celebration day, just like Christmas. They might have been cold back then (with no central heating), but to make up for it, they had a lot more party days than we do now.

Lydia bit her lip. Balls? Parties? In Hopperton they had visited their friends in winter, people she had known all her life, not strangers or fine folk. They had made up poems, played silly games and sang ditties, like the one about the girl who fell into a pot (you had to hear it live to really understand how funny it was). Lydia was frequently asked to perform her impression of a fox walking jauntily through town of a morning (again, live, this was an absolute showstopper). But something told Lydia that parties at Peppomberley were going to be a lot less fun.

She stared at the crumbs of tea cake and remembered how far away summer and strawberries really were.

The back door **burst** open, and a young boy came through – he was Lydia's age but taller and with the same sandy hair as Harriet, and just as covered in freckles.

'Auntie Harriet, Ronalds is shouting about some mess he's found in the hall and I'm telling you now, you better make him a good tea because he is fair grumpy—'

He stopped and stared at Lydia. They both began to apologise at the same time.

'Sorry, miss, I didn't realise—'

'I shouldn't be here, I am supposed to be—'

'Oh me, oh my!' Harriet laughed. 'Bertie, this is Miss Marmalade, the girl Lady Partridge has taken on as a ward and—'

'Please call me Lydia, no one ever called me Miss Marmalade before I arrived here.' Lydia knew she could trust Harriet, that she didn't have to pass a test with *her*.

'As you wish, Miss Lydia.' Harriet smiled warmly. 'And this is Bertie, the stable boy and my nephew, and someone who knows to knock at the window and take mucky boots off before coming in here!'

Colin gave a yip, and Harriet realised he had not been formally introduced.

'Forgive me, Master Colin, this here is Bertie, also a young gentleman in training. But Bertie, you haven't seen him, right?' She **tapped** her nose and **winked** at him.

Bertie nodded and winked back at his aunt and at Lydia. But his smile suddenly dropped as he noticed a familiar face pass the kitchen window. 'Ronalds is coming!'

Somehow Harriet shoved Colin, the blanket bundle and Lydia all into the pantry just as Ronalds opened the back door. The pantry door swung open a crack and Lydia could see Ronalds' face, redder and crosser than ever.

'Unbelievable! The ridiculousness I have endured today!' He **scowled** and walked towards the pantry.

Lydia held her breath and squeezed herself as far back into the cupboard as she could.

'Mister Ronalds, you're needed at the stables. I was sent to fetch you!' Bertie exclaimed.

'Why?' Ronalds sneered at him.

'The – the horses have escaped!'

'All of them?'

'Yes! I think they've learnt how to undo the doors, sir—'

'Oh for goodness' sake.' Ronalds stomped back to the door. 'Quick then, boy!'

Bertie **scurried** after him, giving Harriet a cheeky smile before he closed the door behind him.

Lydia cautiously stepped out of the pantry. She hadn't meant for anyone to find out about Colin and now two people had.

'Don't worry about Bertie,' said Harriet, reading Lydia's mind. 'He's a good egg, he won't say nothing to Ronalds. And I won't either. Colin is clearly a gentleman and it's a pleasure to make his acquaintance!' She gave the dog a **belly rub** and he rolled over like the soft cake he was.

Lydia smiled weakly, but she felt the threat of tears

that had become all too familiar recently. If she'd been caught, Colin would have been taken away. No part of her could endure that, not after everything they'd been through. She had to be more careful.

Harriet reached over and **squeezed** Lydia's hand. The forgotten feeling of a warm palm in her own made her heart ache.

'Now, Miss Lydia, do you know it's the sixth of December today, St Nicholas Day! It's the start of winter proper now. If you look out the window and see a **sprite** today, they have to grant you a wish. It's their present in honour of St Nick and how he's always looked after them.'

'But I know they're not real,' said Lydia. 'Well, my mum used to tell me they were, but I know they're just make-believe.' She understood Harriet was trying to cheer her up, but made-up tales wouldn't help her here.

'Oh, you've seen them, you just haven't known it,' Harriet said confidently. She looked out of the small window on to the bare trees outside. 'You ever seen a branch glittering? That's their wings you're seeing as they rush home. They're all out there, in the woods where they live. Proper sprites round here, Miss Lydia, not nice ones with pretty wings. Winter sprites are mischievous and cheeky and, most of time, very grumpy. Today is the only day they'll grant you a wish, so you might as well try 'cause tomorrow they'll pretend they didn't hear you.'

Lydia felt a swell in her chest. Harriet might be telling her childish stories, but she was doing it to be kind. And Bertie had risked a lot to distract Ronalds. This wasn't her home, but she had a belly full of tea cake, and some new friends, and that was more than she'd had this morning.

'It'll be all right, my love – I don't know how and I don't know why, but it will, it just will.'

And Harriet gave Lydia's hand another squeeze.

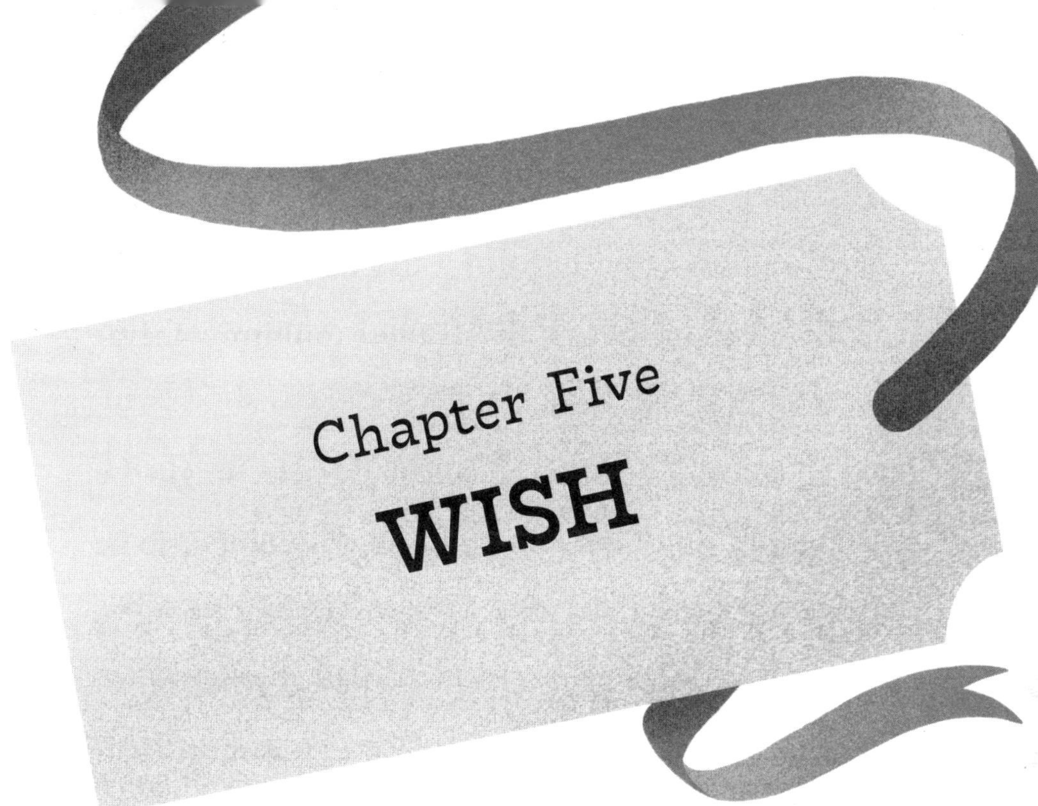

Chapter Five
WISH

Lydia was back in her room, unpacking her few possessions. She hadn't much to bring with her, but one of the most beloved items was her father's old compass. Her mother had explained if Lydia looked at it, she could work out where Hopperton was by following the needle. Lydia knew she was now further north, and the needle would point south to where Hopperton still stood. She carefully took it out and sat on the bed, watching the gold needle move around until it settled.

Lydia looked out of the round window at the darkening sky. The day had been endless: she'd been made to attend a long dull luncheon and then spend a long dull afternoon in the library, with no prospect of investigating the house or even starting to solve the mystery of how her mother had known Lady Partridge.

The sun had set and the thick blanket of clouds drifted away to reveal a deep dark-blue filled with stars. Lydia felt her eyes becoming heavy again. She really was tired and she still had a formal dinner to get through. As she struggled to keep her eyes open, she suddenly thought she saw a bright yellow spark fly past the window. She sat up, her mind still wondering about what Harriet had said about sprites, their wings **glittering**, and wishes – silly talk of course, tales they tell children to cheer them up on dark winter days. And she wasn't a silly child any more.

Still, she opened the window a little. The cold night air rushed in and cooled her cheeks. The light had gone, but well … what harm would it do, making one small wish? What if there *was* a winter sprite? She scrunched her eyes up and spoke out loud to the star-speckled sky. 'I wish my mum was here with me.'

As Lydia spoke the words out loud, she began to cry. Huge, raindrop tears poured down her face and she **sobbed** and **sobbed**. She sat on the bed and grabbed her pillow to muffle the sound. She was scared to admit it, but my goodness, did she miss home, did she miss her mum and how she longed for it to be last summer again when she was as ignorant of Peppomberley as the hedgehogs in Hopperton.

Colin clambered on to her lap and placed his soft cheek next to hers. She held him close, grateful he was with her. Eventually she ran out of tears, and lay curled with her best friend, feeling it was them against the world.

***

After a short time there was a rap at the door and Colin growled. Lydia picked him up and put him in the wardrobe. 'Sssh, Colly!' she begged him.

It was the maid who had greeted her from the carriage. The girl curtseyed, and Lydia tried to memorise how she did it, so she could recreate it later. 'Good evening, Miss Marmalade, I've been sent to dress you for dinner. I'm Martha – we met earlier, when you were talking to your blankets.'

Lydia sensed that Martha wasn't being rude; she was simply reminding Lydia how they had met.

'Er, yes, indeed there are many Hopperton traditions that can seem unusual,' Lydia gently joked, but detected Martha wasn't keen on those either. 'Right … um, Martha, please forgive me, but I've not had a maid before. I used to live in a cottage, and when it was teatime, well, we just washed our hands and sat at the table.' Lydia took a deep breath and tried to hide her embarrassment. She wished she knew more about what a *proper* lady was supposed to do! She would really need Martha's help if she had any chance of impressing Lady Partridge tonight. She heard her mother's words again. *Just be honest, Lydia.* 'I don't know what to wear for dinner in a house as grand as this one.'

Martha **grinned** and clapped her hands. 'I've been waiting for a challenge like this all my life, Miss Marmalade. We need a clean dress and hair brushed and a washed face!'

She marched past Lydia into her bedroom. 'I only have two dresses,' Lydia said, following her. 'I just have this one and the one I wear on special days.' She pointed to a pretty but old dress with little green flowers on it. Her mother had made it for her, and she loved it so much she was loath to admit that recently it had got quite tight on the arms.

Martha **scrunched** her nose. 'Oh, miss, it is not a nice dress.'

'It *is* nice, Martha, it's just—' Lydia tried to hide her hurt feelings. She was going to need a tough skin to survive here.

Martha picked it up and pulled at the seams. 'It will have to do for tonight. I shall speak to Lady Partridge, she gets all her new clothes sent from Bath, so they should send some for you too.'

'Oh, thank you, Martha.'

'I will not pay for it, miss.' Martha clearly took things quite literally.

'Just – that's lovely.'

Once her face had been scrubbed and Martha had brushed and plaited her hair around her head in a way Lydia assumed was fashionable, Martha looked her up and down. 'You look fine, miss. Not nice, but better,' she said matter-of-factly.

Lydia went to say thank you but stopped herself.

'I agree,' she said firmly.

'I'll be back when it's time for dinner,' said Martha, before walking briskly out of the room and shutting the door.

Lydia sighed deeply as she looked back at her reflection again, this time her hair having been fully tamed. It would take some getting used to seeing herself like this, becoming the person Lady Partridge wanted her to be. But what choice did she have? She had to pass the test, or else she'd **lose everything** she had left.

For a second, Lydia heard a faint ripple of bells – but that left her mind as she smelt burning. She checked the candles, but there was nothing untoward. She looked at the grate. There was a small fire laid there but it wasn't lit – although at that moment, Lydia could have sworn she saw a spark leap from inside it.

She stepped closer and peered into the grate. There, undeniably, was a tiny person, who currently had their bum in the air whilst shouting at something in the logs. Lydia **froze** and blinked again. It was actually a girl, but minute and wearing a skirt made of actual flames. She had bright-red, wild curly hair and delicate see-through wings.

Lydia could see the creature was **tugging** at something that appeared to be **wedged** between two logs.

'A more stupid wand I never did see in all my days! Shaped like a star so it gets stuck in all things!' The creature was pulling on the wand, furious with it. 'Call yourself a wand! You're not a wand, you're a stick with aspirations! You *long* to be a wand!'

Lydia shut her eyes, sure she was imagining things – but when she opened her eyes again, the little creature was still there, seemingly oblivious to her presence. Harriet's voice played back to Lydia. *They're all out there, in the woods where they live … Today is the only day they'll grant you a wish.*

Could it possibly be a … *sprite*? But sprites weren't real – were they?

The girl, who was about the size of a small bird, finally pulled her wand free, the force of which sent her flying out of the grate. She landed with a soft *thump* on the rug, coming face-to-face with Lydia. She immediately jumped up and pointed her wand at Lydia, who **gasped**, expecting something dreadful to happen.

'Oh, woodiculous!' the creature shouted, banging her wand against the hearth, causing sparks to fly from it. 'I only just had it fixed by Keith in the big oak tree, and he's normally very reliable – but *blinking berries and hollyhocks*, this wand has had it!' She threw it to the floor and **stamped** her foot. Sparks cascaded out of it and singed the rug and the sprite.

Lydia tried to take in what was happening in front of her. The tiny girl's hair crackled and occasionally flames jumped out from the top of her head. Upon her feet were little red shoes, but one was bigger than the other and was slipping about a lot (Lydia noticed it was tied to her foot with a piece of dry grass). Her wand was a stick with a **huge** star at the top of it, made of other twigs tied together. It sparked a little, but it seemed to be spluttering too, as if it was running out of energy somehow.

'What *are* you?' Lydia finally whispered.

The creature looked confused. 'Me? You don't know who I am?'

Lydia shook her head, some part of her still not believing what she was seeing.

The creature sighed, pointing at Lydia. 'You gooseberry fool! You wished on a winter sprite, on St Nicholas Day – you *called* me!'

'I didn't – I didn't know sprites were real!' Lydia said.

'Oh well, that's charming – what am I, a chopped apple?! I am real, I am a winter sprite, and my name is Belamina Frosty Wonderlandus Sharp-Leaf, since you didn't ask! But everyone calls me Bel.'

'I'm Lydia Marmalade—'

'And now I have a wish on my hands! This is why they always say "Bel, don't go out on St Nick's Day! Don't do it, Bel!" But do I listen? I'm my own worst blueberry, I really am.' She folded her arms crossly.

'I think I know a little about you. Harriet told me—'

'Oh, you're a friend of Harriet's?' Bel softened. 'She's a good egg. She leaves the acorn cups out for us all winter. A good egg and true.'

Lydia tried a smile, wanting to get on to Bel's good side, if she had one. 'It's nice to meet you. I've never met a sprite before.'

'*Winter* sprite!' Bel huffed. 'As behind the times as a frost in March, are we? Winter sprites are very important, we help all the animals and creatures in the woods during winter, when the Earth is at its coldest and darkest. We can summon warmth and give hope in the dark, when you need it most – but mostly we're not that keen on doing it because it's hard work and you're always cold. We're meant to check in on everyone, but there's a lot more animals these days. I'll be honest, the job has got a lot more paperwork-heavy. Standards have slipped a bit. Look, we do our best, OK?'

'Yes of course,' said Lydia, not knowing what she was agreeing with.

'A few years ago – well, eight hundred and forty-two years ago to be precise, the foxes and badgers actually got together to complain about us not turning up when we said we would. Truth be told, it got quite nasty. So Nick, sorry, St Nicholas, well he's a saint, he really is, he got involved and smoothed it all over. The animals agreed to be more understanding of our time constraints and, to show our thanks to Nick for helping us, we agreed that on the sixth of December, any human who saw a winter sprite could make a wish and we would grant it. But it was a lot of effort and, after a time, winter sprites stopped going out on that night – then we wouldn't have to grant a wish, you see, and Nick sort of let it slide too and … are you following this?' Bel suddenly turned to Lydia.

Lydia nodded, despite her definitely not following anything Bel had said.

'Anyway,' continued Bel, 'eventually humans forgot about us and the St Nick's night wish thing, but I suppose there's a few like Harriet that still remember.'

'But why *did* you go out tonight?' Lydia asked.

'I needed some milk,' Bel said. Lydia waited for more but there didn't seem to be more coming.

Lydia held her breath. She hadn't thought that tonight would have any goodness in it at all, but now her heart was beating with hope. Would Bel be able to make her **wish** come true? Could she see her mother again?

Bel was adjusting the star on her wand, turning it over in her hands. She **banged** it on the fireplace and a large *pop* sounded. Lydia suddenly felt very warm, as if she was standing too near a fire.

'There we go!' Bel shouted and ran towards Lydia, closing her eyes and drawing the wand over her head. Lydia could hear her chanting something faintly under her breath. The sparks on her skirt began to dance as the flames changed colour from orange to red, rising higher until they seemed to cover her whole body. Bel pointed her wand at Lydia, who gripped her fists, bracing herself and closing her eyes—

Then, something happened and Lydia was back in August, the last summer with her mum.

They were walking along the river holding hands, talking about all the shades of green around them, their joint favourite colour. Was grass green better than apple green, or was grasshopper green better than toad green? Lydia smiled at the memory. She could see her mother's long brown hair pinned, but messily tumbling down her back just as Lydia's did. Her mum looked down and smiled, and there it was, the warmth of her love flowing towards Lydia. Now she knew how cold the winter would be without her mum, she longed to stay right here, in the summer, for as long as she could.

But the memory was fading. Lydia reluctantly opened her eyes and saw the dark blue outside the window, and Bel staring at her wand, confused and furious.

'Hedge spikes! It must be broken!' The colour of Bel's skirt dimmed to a pale yellow, like the yolk in an unhappy hen's egg.

Lydia heard a *whack*. And then many *whacks*. Bel was **bashing** the wand over and over again on the floor and shouting, 'Swell-bellied hogs' dripping!' She threw it as hard as she could at the fire. The wand bounced off the fireplace, hit the wooden floor and bounced again, straight into Bel's head, knocking her over flat on her back with her feet in the air.

'Balderdash and blackberries!' Bel shouted. 'I have had it up to here with that wand! I am telling you,

Lydia Marmalade, it's not worth the beech it's made of, I should've got oak! They all said to me, "Get oak, Bel," but no, I had to be different!'

Lydia began to worry about how **loud** she was being. Martha would be back soon. 'Could you maybe be a little quieter, Bel?' The sprite glared at her. 'It's just, I'm already in some trouble—'

'Trouble?' Bel stopped. 'What do you mean?'

'Well.' Lydia struggled to hold all the things that had happened today. 'I'm supposed to be behaving myself and I wasn't supposed to bring Colin here, and Lady Partridge – I'm her ward – is going to throw me out if I don't start behaving like a *proper* lady. And I don't know what that is, but I know I'm not very good at it. If they find out there's an angry sprite made of fire in my room, it might be considered more trouble?'

Bel seemed to take this all in and then said, 'Who's Colin?'

Lydia opened the wardrobe and a little black nose appeared followed by a cross-looking Colin. He *had* been in there a long time, to be fair.

'Ah, Colin! A pleasure,' said Bel, and she shook his paw so confidently, Colin found himself letting out a yip to say hello back.

'Right!' said Bel. 'Back to wishes. You wished that your mother was here with you, yes?'

'Yes,' agreed Lydia, 'But I know that can't happen – Mum's not exactly nearby—'

'That's it!' interrupted Bel. 'That's the reason it's not working properly! Oh, *wand.* I'm all apologies, please take my sincerest mistletoe kisses, you are a *good* wand!' She picked up the wand and **kissed** the star. 'I thought your mother was nearby, Lydia, and the wand would just bring her to us. But if she's further away, that's a different matter. Truth be told, Lydia, I have not done big magic for some time. I mean, if a badger wants a new room in his sett or a fox wants a fluffier tail, that's easy – but bringing a whole person to us, *especially* if they're far away, is a bit trickier.'

Bel paused, deep in thought. 'If I can do your wish, then I can get back home. My pal Stanley is waiting for me. He's a squirrel, but one of the all right ones.'

'The thing is, Bel,' said Lydia quietly. 'My mum's not here because she ... passed away.'

'Where did she go passing?' asked Bel.

Lydia swallowed hard. 'She's dead, Bel. She died.'

'Oh,' said Bel. 'Lydia, there's no magic that can make someone alive again. That must be why your wish is stuck.'

Lydia **blinked** back tears. She already knew what she had wished for was **impossible**, but, just for a moment, she had wished, had hoped, that something extraordinary might happen. Now she felt empty and foolish.

'Tree stumps and thorns!' declared Bel. 'Nice to meet you, Lydia Marmalade, and sorry for all the faff, and all the whatnots. I can't help you with that wish, so I'll be off. Stanley gets the right hump if I'm late. Merry winter!'

Lydia watched dumbfounded as Bel unfurled her wings and flew towards the window, pointing her wand. The semi-circle of glass swung open and Bel **disappeared** into the night sky, leaving a trail of yellow sparks hanging in the air.

***

There was a sharp knock at the door.

'Miss Lydia, it's time for dinner,' Martha's voice called. Lydia stared at Colin and threw a blanket over him.

'I'll be back as soon as I can!' she whispered. Lydia looked at the open window one last time, before opening the door and stepping into the corridor.

She was dreading dinner. But she reminded herself that she still had a mystery to solve. How had her mum known Lady Partridge? If only she could find something out during dinner, she might feel as if she belonged in this draughty old house.

She followed Martha, who was already giving her a

detailed summary of all the different plates they used during dinner at Peppomberley.

'A side plate is much smaller, miss, hence its ability to be at the side …'

It was going to be a **long** evening.

Chapter Six

ST NICHOLAS'S DINNER

Lydia thought she couldn't be more overwhelmed at the grandness of Peppomberley's rooms, but she had not yet seen the **huge** drawing room where Lady Partridge received her guests. It was pale yellow, with a small pianoforte in the corner, and what seemed like a large number of people. On a large golden sofa Lydia saw a well-dressed young man who she recognised from the corridor as Edmund Partridge. Next to him on an armchair was a very short woman whose legs were dangling down and who looked deeply uncomfortable in a bright green dress. It was the colour of vomit, truth be told, and Lydia instantly added it to her list of greens as the winner of worst green. Lydia realised the lady was talking to Edmund, but he didn't seem to be doing any talking back.

'Lord Partridge,' said the lady, 'you cannot find anyone these days with a good knowledge of shells. I myself have many different types of shell, and let me tell you they are all—'

Seeing Lydia, Edmund stood up and crossed the room to her, clearly keen to escape the shells.

'Greetings, Miss Lydia Marmalade,' he said stiffly. 'You are welcome to Peppomberley. I have heard not nearly enough about you, given that you are joining my household.' He shot Lady Partridge a look. 'However, the most important thing is, can you sing for us?'

Lydia tried to think of something ladylike to say, but the truth seemed safer. 'I can, but it's not the nicest sound, sir. My neighbours said what I made up for in volume I lost in tune.'

Edmund laughed, giving Lydia a surprised look. 'Well, I shall play the piano if someone will sing. And if you do not recommend yourself, then it must be our most famous of sweet voices, Miss Marianne Braun?'

It was then that Lydia saw her. Marianne. The girl who Harriet said Lady Partridge wanted to marry her son. She had a beautiful white dress, covered with delicate gold embroidery; her dark blonde hair was plaited and swirled over her head, and there was an air of elegance about her that Lydia had never seen in anyone before. So that is what a 'proper lady' should look like, Lydia thought, her heart sinking as she looked down at her too-tight dress, scuffed shoes and hair she could already feel was unravelling.

Edmund approached Marianne, and Lydia noticed how well they looked together, his dark curly hair with her golden hue: it was like the sun and the moon meeting. Lydia was still a little wary of Edmund – was he as strict as his mother, Lady Partridge?

He sat down at the piano and began to play a carol, as Marianne sang in a language that Lydia did not recognise. Her voice was high and beautifully clear, like birdsong. Lydia **disappeared** into the music, allowing the notes to wrap themselves around her, when she felt a tug at her elbow. It was the short green lady. 'That's my daughter, of course,' she said proudly. 'I'm Lady Agatha Braun, and you must be Miss Lydia Marmalade?'

'Yes, ma'am,' said Lydia, remembering she must try to be polite and think about appropriate conversation for such an occasion. But she needn't have worried, for Lady Braun did not need any help on her specialist subject.

'Why only last week I added the rarest shell to my collection. I said to my sister, this shell cannot have been found on Brighton beach! Her shell collection is of five hundred and two pieces, you understand, mine is of nearly six hundred, I think I would know a shell that is in fact from the Kent coastal area when I saw it …'

Lydia let her mind drift away on the music, knowing her silence was the best companion for Lady Braun.

The carol ended and everyone clapped, including Lady Partridge, who appeared to be enjoying herself, which was not something Lydia had seen before.

Marianne caught sight of Lydia and headed in her direction. Lydia **stiffened**. She caught eyes with Lady Partridge, who was giving her a very serious **'behave yourself'** look. Marianne grabbed both Lydia's hands and tugged her away from Lady Braun, who didn't seem to notice that she'd lost her audience and was happily still talking to no one about her largest conch shell.

'Oh Miss Marmalade! What a pleasure it is to meet you! How strange you must feel leaving your home and arriving here. I cannot imagine what you've been through!'

Lydia felt **dizzy** at her kindness. 'Yes, it is very strange indeed, Miss Braun.'

'Call me Marianne, please. We shall be as sisters.' She smiled. 'Allow me to speak truthfully, dearest Lydia. Peppomberley is such a grand house indeed, being here can seem not unlike entering a hedge maze you did not realise you had fallen into.'

Lydia laughed and tried to quiet herself as Lady Partridge stared over at them both.

'Yes,' Lydia confided, 'a maze in which I am nowhere near the centre and in danger of being marched to the exit at any minute!'

'They would never, Lydia, I will not let them!' Marianne said earnestly.

Lydia smiled gratefully.

'You need something in your hair to match this dress,' said Marianne, plucking one of the long ostrich feathers that bobbed atop her own head and tucking it into Lydia's simple plait. 'There, now you are a Peppomberley lady!'

Lydia blushed. Marianne's **kindness** was almost too much to bear after all the worry of the day. A bell rang out and everyone stood up. Marianne squeezed Lydia's hand. 'To the centre of the maze! Follow me.'

The party headed into a magnificent dining room. The **huge** table was swallowed up by fruits and candies and meats and china tureen pots with large metal ladles sticking out of them, and, in the centre, a huge seven-tier cake. Lydia had to stifle a giggle, remembering Colin happily tucking into the sponge of the intended eighth tier. It really was a **magnificent** cake, perfectly iced, with delicate green leaves winding their way around all seven layers up to the top, where real rose leaves had been arranged around a large pink rose made of sugar.

Marianne kept hold of her arm and sat Lydia down

beside her, Edmund joined them next, sitting on the other side of Marianne, while Lady Partridge and Lady Braun entered slowly in their stiff dresses and high headpieces. The rest of the guests seemed to know one another and naturally found their seats.

The dinner began with a white soup and Lydia tried hard to control her hand, which wouldn't stop trembling. She was so worried she would spill something and fail her first test in front of Lady Partridge.

When everyone had finished eating, the table was completely cleared and the tablecloth removed to reveal another tablecloth. There was quite a long pause while they had to put everything back on the table and then the next course was served, pork and root vegetables. The food was so tasty, Lydia had to remind herself not to mop up her plate with a slice of bread, as she would have done at home.

She picked up a fork and instantly heard Marianne emit a small cough. She swiftly placed the fork back on the table, looking up to see Lady Partridge frowning. Why were there fork rules?! It would take a miracle for Lydia to pass as a lady in these few weeks. She found the right fork and tucked in.

Lady Braun suddenly stood up, although she was so short that standing up didn't equate with the effect she had hoped for and everyone carried on with their conversation.

Lady Partridge stood too and there was an

immediate hush. 'Ah, Lady Braun, I see you have some special words for us that I'm sure we will find most diverting.'

'Thank you, Lady Partridge. What pleasure we take in spending time with our good neighbours and we are grateful to the new Lord Partridge for providing such pleasant company. We have worn all our finery for the occasion – as you see, my dear Marianne is wearing a new ruby necklace, gifted from her great-uncle in Germany. It is quite the sight, is it not, Lord Partridge?'

He blushed the colour of rubies and simply nodded.

Marianne smoothed things over. 'Mama is too proud of such a gem, but I am grateful to wear something equal to this house's charms.' She smiled at Edmund, and he blushed past red and into purple.

'And *expensive*!' Lady Braun chipped in.

Thankfully the servants entered to clear the table, and bring some delicious baked apples that smelt like winter itself – nutmeg, cinnamon and star anise rose out of the bowls and into everyone's nostrils. *Harriet has done a wonderful job*, thought Lydia.

Lydia was exhausted but relieved. The dinner was nearly over and no one had paid her much attention, just as Lady Partridge had wanted. Soon she would be able to go back to her room and hug Colin. It had been a long and strange day – not least because of the sprite in her room. Although now Lydia wondered whether she had seen the sprite at all. Perhaps she had been so desperate to see her mum again that maybe she'd just imagined it all?

Then she saw it. In the centre of the table stood an ornate fruit bowl, full of sugared fruits and nuts, and from behind them, a flurry of yellow sparks appeared. There was Bel, tugging on a huge pear with both hands and huffing about it. With one big pull, the stalk came off and she went somersaulting underneath the table.

Lydia held her breath. Surely someone must have seen the sprite? But the conversation went on. Lydia could see where Bel must be walking under the table as, one by one, the guests opposite her started to fan themselves with the unexpected warmth. What could she do?

Wanting to appear *proper*, Lydia placed a spoonful of the apples into her mouth and let herself be comforted by the warm, sweet fruit. Harriet had cooked it with blackcurrants, and it had turned a deep red. Lydia picked up her bowl to scrape as much of the lovely pudding as possible on to her spoon.

But the sound of paws on a wooden floor stopped her in her tracks. That was Colin! He must have escaped … and was now racing along the corridor towards the dining room! Simultaneously, she could feel Bel tugging at her dress, and her feet feeling as hot as if she was plunging them in a bath.

Lydia **sprang** out of her seat, forgetting the bowl in her hand, and watched in horror as the remains of her bright apple and berry juice **splattered** all over Marianne's white dress.

Marianne let out a **cry** of shock, but not as loud as her mother, who screamed in horror, tried to rise, then fell off her chair. Edmund moved to assist Marianne, but at the same time so did Lydia, and so they cracked heads. Edmund clung to his skull, glaring at Lydia. There were shocked gasps from all around the table, as Colin **burst** into the room, then ran around barking at everyone and licking up bits of baked apple from Marianne's dress.

Lydia tried to ignore the ringing in her ears and appeal to Lady Partridge, to tell her how sorry she was, but she refused to meet Lydia's eyes and instead rapped firmly on the table to quell the chaos.

A silence fell over the guests, apart from Lady Braun who was still huffing and puffing as she hoisted herself back on to her seat, no one having come to her aid. By now all her feathers were pointing down and her hair was quite as messy as Lydia's always looked.

Lydia couldn't breathe. Colin! Loose! This was her

fault. She had to try and fix it. She scooped up Colin. **'Please, Lady Partridge, I—'**

'Enough, child!' Lady Partridge's cold expression made it quite clear her appeal was pointless. She then mustered a smile for Marianne. 'Miss Braun, I must apologise—'

'Oh, there is no need!' Marianne interrupted cheerfully, 'I am quite well, indeed I have a new colour to my dress, which now matches my necklace!' Everyone smiled, thankful for the lighter mood.

'You are too kind, Miss Braun,' said Lady Partridge, rapping on the table and calling, 'Ronalds!' He instantly appeared from the hallway. 'We appear to have a dog in the house, despite what was agreed with Miss Marmalade. Please release it into the woods tonight.'

Colin heard her tone of voice and wriggled free of Lydia's grasp before **darting** out of the room as fast as lightning.

'Please, Lady Partridge!' cried Lydia. 'I know you are furious with me, but it is not Colin's fault, I should not have brought him with me, it's true, but I could not bear to leave him, he is my best friend and—'

Lady Partridge silenced her with a raised hand. 'It seems you are most tired, dear child, it is time for you to go to your room. Ronalds?' He stepped towards Lydia, whose heart was beating so fast she felt her head go light.

'Dear Lady Partridge, is that delightful dog a pet?' Marianne asked unexpectedly.

Lady Partridge composed herself before answering. 'Indeed, it is not *my* pet, Miss Braun. I am not fond of wild animals inside a house – especially not in such a house as Peppomberley.' Lydia sensed if anyone other than Marianne had spoken Lady Partridge would have chucked them out the window by now.

'Do tell me what breed it is, Miss Marmalade,' said Marianne, turning to face Lydia. 'Why my mama and I had the sweetest dog in London, Wilhelm, and I do miss him so!'

Lydia tried to think carefully and slow her words. 'A sausage dog! He is called Colin. I rescued him when he was a pup. Someone tried to leave him by a pond, but he actually likes swimming and jumps into lakes at any opportunity!' She didn't dare look at Lady Partridge, or at Bel, who was now hiding in the antlers of a deer head on the wall. They were starting to smoulder.

'Oh, what a charming chap! Tell me, Lady Partridge, does your cook have a dog? Our cook used to be so grumpy until we got Wilhelm. He proved himself most useful, keeping rats out of the chicken coop, so we always had plenty of fresh eggs and he must have softened Cook's heart as her food was even more delicious after he arrived! I do believe a dog brings a heart to a home, don't you agree?'

The whole table waited for Lady Partridge to reply.

Lydia plucked up the courage to look at her mistress and could see her **nostrils flaring**, although her smile never faltered.

'Why Miss Braun, what a wife you will make a gentleman one day, you are as thoughtful as a person can be.'

'Can anyone else smell venison cooking?' said Lady Braun to herself.

Lydia knew Lady Partridge was furious. How had she ruined everything so quickly? Her first test as a 'proper lady' had been to cause *no trouble at all* and it would be fair to say she had absolutely **failed**.

'Perhaps Ronalds may enquire if Cook is in need of a dog. If he stays he must be useful, of course.' Lady Partridge's hand was gripping her glass so tight her knuckles were white.

Lydia noticed that Marianne's hand was shaking a little. Clearly she had been more nervous than she had seemed. Lydia wished she could say thank you, but she knew that would be a step too far.

'And now,' added Lady Partridge, 'I must insist it is time for Lydia to rest. What an eventful first day you have had.' She gave Ronalds a nod.

Lydia walked around the table towards the door, her feet feeling like lead weights. As she passed behind Lady Partridge a cold hand gripped her wrist. She could feel her breath in her ear. 'Pack your bags, Miss Marmalade,' she whispered. 'Your carriage will be waiting in the morning.'

Chapter Seven
GOODBYES

Lydia's bedroom door was open, and she could hear Colin **whimpering** in shame. How had he got out earlier? Bel! She must have magicked the door open. Ronalds strode forwards, but Lydia burst out, 'No! I will get him, please, he is my dog and I am still a guest here, even if I do leave tomorrow!'

Ronalds looked a little taken aback. He sneered at her, but he stepped aside.

Lydia went into her room and shut the door

in Ronalds' face.

It was absolute **chaos**, from ceiling to floor. The mattress had been dragged off the bed, the wardrobe was open, the wash bowl upturned, all her possessions and books were scattered on the floor.

'Colin! What on earth?' cried Lydia.

From under a pillow, Colin emerged, running to her and wrapping himself round her ankles. Lydia bent down and stroked his warm body. 'What happened?' Colin merely looked up at her and then hung his long nose down.

Suddenly Lydia smelt burning and scanned the room. Standing on the chair was Bel! Her skirt still aflame and sparking, trying to break open a pine cone. *Bel was real. Sprites were real.*

'Oh my sticks! I'm starved through like a woodlouse with no wood! Oh, bluebell bulbs and daisy chains, do you have some nibbles? I didn't get a chance to grab anything from that dining room.'

Ronalds rapped on the door angrily. 'Marmalade! What are you doing?'

Lydia hadn't much time. She would deal with Bel later. Now, she had to say goodbye to Colin. He seemed already to know what was happening and had gathered his favourite blanket and was standing by the door looking pained but trying to be brave.

'Oh Col, Lord Colamin Coldrop the Third of Colllington! I'm so sorry. I tried my best, I really did, but it didn't work, I knew I'd fail the test, just not this soon. But for now, you will have a home with Harriet, so at least there'll be plenty of cake for you!' Colin began to wag his tail. 'All right, don't be too pleased to leave me,' Lydia said. 'But you must be good and listen and not get in the way.'

Colin gave a nod to say he understood the seriousness of the mission and was prepared to accept it. Lydia wrapped him up, took a small date out of her pocket that she had smuggled from dinner for him, and tucked that in too.

'I will come and see you as soon as possible, somehow. I promise.' He gave her a lick on the nose and placed his head on her shoulder gently. Lydia turned to the sprite. 'Now, Bel, hide right this minute!' Bel's skirt flickered as if she was blowing out a candle and she scurried under the bed.

Lydia opened the door. Ronalds jumped back, his ear having clearly been pressed up against it trying to eavesdrop.

'He likes milk and bread in the morning and the clang of pans can make him nervous, so please warn Harriet to put things down on surfaces gently.'

Ronalds could barely contain his sneer. 'He shall get crumbs when they are to be spared and he shall sleep outside, Miss Marmalade. He is a dog, not a royal prince.' He took Colin off her **roughly** and Lydia stared at her beloved friend until Ronalds had **disappeared** down the corridor.

***

Lydia closed the door and stood still. Colin was safe, but for how long? Her mind **whirred** with the evening's mayhem, and then there was the horror of tomorrow looming. Would she really be sent to the workhouse?

'Hollyspikes! Someone should really dust under there!' Bel coughed as she emerged from under the bed.

'Bel! You are real! Why did you come back? And why is my room upside down?'

Bel looked **sheepish** and **folded** her arms. 'I did try and go home, Lydia Marmalade, I did, but, well … I couldn't.' She managed to **wrench** off a piece of pine cone and began to chew on it.

'You couldn't?'

'No! I couldn't! Stanley was making an acorn crumble, too. I don't *want* to be here, obviously! Every time I tried to fly away – well, it wouldn't work.'

'What happened?'

'When I got close to the woods I got tugged back, as though a rope were pulling me back to you and there was nothing I could do to stop it. I ran at it a few times, like a hedgehog after a worm, before I realised it must be the wish. There's a connection between us that can't be broken. You'll probably feel a pull if you try to go too far from me, too. I'm beholden to you, until it's granted. I can only go where you go!'

'Oh, Bel,' Lydia sighed.

'Worst thing is, I invited people over at the weekend, so they'll all turn up and not have a clue why I'm not there. I bought a load of quiches in too, so they'll go off.'

'Oh gosh, I really am sorry.'

'And my pal Flo is having a big ball for midwinter and I had a new hat to wear, made of snowdrop buds that I'd grown special. AND I won't get my magic back if I don't grant your impossible wish! It's a wish-tastrophe! What's a winter sprite without no magic? I'll be like – like a badger without its stripe, a fox without its tail, Jack Frost without his sense of entitlement!'

Bel **slumped** down on the floor and threw her bit of pine cone at the fireplace.

It bounced off the grate and hit her on the head. 'Hazelnuts!' she shouted.

Lydia thought back to yesterday when she was still in her home, when she still had Colin, when she didn't know sprites existed. All she had wanted was to have her mother with her again, but now she'd caused more trouble than she ever thought possible! She had bound Bel to her, lost Colin – and now, what would become of her? She let her body slump to the floor too and leant against the door, her head in her hands.

There was a **long silence** and then, 'So, where is your ma then?' asked Bel.

Lydia sat up and sighed. 'She's dead, Bel. I did already tell you that.'

'I'm sorry, Miss Lydia, that's right rubbish.'

Lydia smiled. 'Yes, it is. Right rubbish.'

'But where *is* she? When sprites get really old they go off to the summer wood.'

'A wood?'

'Oh yes, it's lovely, it's always summer, it's filled with buttercups and bluebells and every apple tree is always laden with fruit, and the blackberries are ripe all year round. The grass is filled with moss and is soft beneath your feet and if you press your nose to it, it smells of earth and warmth all the time.'

'Sounds wonderful,' Lydia smiled. 'Can you go there?'

'No. I don't know when I'll go, but I don't feel ready yet. When you're ready to go, you go.'

Lydia stared at her. 'Humans don't always know when it's time to go and sometimes it happens far too soon, like my mum. I'm not sure where she is, I pray to her in heaven, but,' she paused, 'but where I feel her the most is in here.' Lydia placed her hand across her heart.

Lydia scooted across to Bel, got another date out of her pocket and handed it to her. 'Bel – I think I need your help.'

'Blizzarding periwinkles! You need *my* help? How can I help you? I'm just a winter sprite, and I'm going to lose all my magic if I can't grant this wish!' She pointed her wand into the air – a small flurry of sparks came out, and Lydia noticed Bel had changed Lydia's shoes from scuffed and tired to bright gold. 'By Jove, got a little bit left in there!' Bel said, laughing. Lydia could hear a tiny ripple of bells, as if from a long way away.

She took a **big breath**. In the fairy stories her mother had told her when she was little, wishes could sometimes come true in strange and surprising ways. Maybe they just needed to think about the wish differently?

She thought again about what she had asked for. *I wish my mum was here with me.* The glimmerings of an idea came to her. It might not work, but it was worth a try, she knew that.

'Bel, I have a feeling there's something **mysterious** happening at Peppomberley. Lady Partridge seems to know things about my mother, so they must have known each other, or at least met. Maybe I can find out more about my mother's past, something that will make me feel closer to her, like she's here with me – and *that* will make the wish come true.' Bel frowned and Lydia rushed on. 'We can't give up! If we search for clues, try to figure out what happened in the past … maybe that will solve both our troubles.'

Bel looked at her. **'This sounds like shenanigans.'**

'Yes, I suppose it will be.'

Bel smiled, the cheekiest grin Lydia had ever seen. 'Oh, I'm an expert in those, Miss Lydia!'

Chapter Eight
GOOD MORNING

The early sun was pale yellow and as it came through the curtains, Lydia had her repeated sensation where she thought she was back home in Hopperton, expecting to see the low ceiling of her bedroom and hear her mother singing downstairs …

I remember my true love,
You've been there all my life,

And I'll remember my true love,
Till the days meet the tide.

She blinked again, saw the large wooden wardrobe and felt the coarse blanket curled around her feet. She was still in Peppomberley. She stared at the high ceiling, marvelling at how much space one house could have above everyone's heads. But big houses didn't make people happy. *Happiness falls where it wants, no matter how fine your purse is.*

The smell of burning pulled her from her thoughts and everything that had happened yesterday came flooding back. Leaving home, that awful dinner, losing Colin. Lydia took a long shaky breath and sat up to find Bel standing on her belly. Oh yes, and she'd also discovered yesterday that sprites were real.

'Oh, it wakes, does it?' Bel had her arms folded and was pursing her lips as if she had sucked a lemon.

'Bel, I just need to—'

'You need to get up, Lady Nightshade! It's past morning and past breakfast, surely!'

Lydia swung her legs out of bed. 'I have to get dressed and find Colin. He'll be so worried. And then I have to convince Lady Partridge to let me stay, even though it's awful here. If I don't I'll never solve the mystery, I'll never see Colin again and you'll never get your magic back.'

Lydia pulled on her dress and stockings and tried to gather her unruly brown hair into something that looked less large and hedge-like.

'You're right, Lyds,' said Bel. 'I'm coming with you!' She started climbing up Lydia's dress, heading towards the pocket.

'But what if you burn my dress? Your sparks?'

'Stop fretting, you sound like a panicky pigeon!' Bel muttered something and the sparks on her skirt **extinguished**.

Lydia took a deep breath in, felt her ribs expand and settle. She had no plan whatsoever, but she knew one thing. Being sent away and **abandoning** Colin just couldn't happen. She would not let it. If she could survive the last few months, she could get through today. She needed to think clearly (and try to accept she had a sprite in her pocket).

There was a knock at her door and the handle turned. Martha came in briskly. 'Lady Partridge wishes to see you, miss, she is in her drawing room.'

Lydia picked up her mother's blue shawl and wrapped it around her. She desperately wanted to see Colin, but she must see Lady Partridge first. She must think of some way to convince her to let them stay.

Bel began to wriggle so Lydia gave a little jump to

try and hide her **twitching** pocket. Martha stared at her, frowning.

'I always jump before breakfast! Helps the digestion.'

'They do things differently in Hopperton, miss.'

Lydia felt a warmth in her pocket and saw yellow sparks coming out of it. Suddenly, her pocket was filled with walnuts, which began to spill out all over the floor. Martha looked more confused than Lydia had ever seen her look.

'Oh gosh, I took some walnuts last night to nibble on and I must've forgotten!' Lydia tried to laugh it off, reaching into her pocket to give Bel a flick.

'But we didn't have no walnuts last night ...' Martha said, staring open-mouthed as they dropped out of Lydia's pocket, leaving a trail back to her bedroom.

***

Lydia entered the drawing room to find Lady Partridge at her desk. She looked up and cast an **icy gaze** at Lydia.

'Good morning, ma'am.' She tried to be confident, but her hands were trembling. She felt Bel give her a kick on her thigh. 'What a fine morning it is today.'

'Yes, I'm sure a carriage journey will be most enjoyable in such weather.'

'I brought you some walnuts.' Lydia sheepishly placed a huge pile of them on to the desk. 'Lady Partridge, I'm so very sorry for—'

'For what? Bringing the dog in spite of the fact I told you not to? Lying to me? Embarrassing me at an important dinner?' Lady Partridge's voice was slow and controlled. Lydia felt herself trembling. *Be brave, be brave.*

'For all of those things, Lady Partridge! I am grateful that Colin will be allowed to stay in the kitchen. If you give me another chance, I promise I will become exactly the sort of young lady who belongs at Peppomberley.

And I will never, ever lie to you again.'

Lady Partridge began to tidy away her papers furiously. 'I am not known for going back on my word, Miss Marmalade!' She paused and turned away from Lydia. '*Proper* ladies do not spend time in the kitchens. They do not speak unless they are spoken to. And they do *not* cause trouble.' Lady Partridge drew breath and Lydia was sure she saw something in her face besides anger – a look of **surprising emotion**. 'Against my better judgement, you may have one final opportunity to prove yourself a proper young lady. But if you ever lie to me again or fail to behave with decorum, you will be sent straight to the workhouse!'

'Thank you, Lady Partridge. I won't let you down.' Lydia said, and was **surprised** at how much she actually meant it.

Ronalds appeared at the door, 'Announcing Miss Marianne Braun!' He saw Lydia. 'Shall I fetch the carriage, ma'am?'

Lady Partridge looked at Lydia.

'No. Not today, Ronalds.'

He stood open-mouthed, not even attempting to hide his shock.

'Thank you, Ronalds!' Lady Partridge added sharply. 'See Miss Braun in.'

Lydia's heart **lifted** to see her friend. Marianne ran to her and greeted her as warmly as if they had known each other for many years, not one night. 'Oh, Miss Marmalade, I am glad to see you, I was passing the house and I came in to invite the whole household to our Midwinter Ball next week. I would so love to see everyone from Peppomberley there.'

Lady Partridge winced a little as she realised Marianne was inviting Lydia as well.

'Miss Marmalade is far too young for such occasions, my dear.'

'Oh, in the country, I'm sure she is old enough to attend.'

'Indeed. But the girl has nothing to wear, as you can see.'

She gestured to Lydia's dress, which Lydia thought was a bit unnecessary. She wanted to say something, but she knew the ice she was on was so paper thin she could see the bottom of the lake underneath her feet.

'That is indeed no problem at all! I have so many dresses I no longer wear that I'm sure will fit Miss Marmalade.'

Lydia smiled gratefully.

'You could not be asked to share such precious treasured possessions,' Lady Partridge remarked with concern.

'Not at all, she is most welcome. For shame the good lady that hangs on to clothing that no longer serves her when someone else is cold and in need.' Marianne cast her most dazzling smile at Lady Partridge, who returned the gesture.

Lydia had no idea what was actually going on, but the air rippled with tension like a chess game.

And then Bel jabbed her in the leg.

'Ooh! Owww—' Lydia cried.

Both Marianne and Lady Partridge stared at her.

'Oww-hhh … while shepherds watched their flocks by night!' she started singing, and she really wished she hadn't. Lady Partridge looked even more enraged, but Marianne grinned from ear to ear, 'Oh, Miss Marmalade, that is one of my most treasured festive carols. May we sing it together at the Midwinter Ball?' Marianne looked at Lady Partridge for permission, whose face was now locked in a tight sort of smile-grimace.

'I'm sure to hear you both would be a delight indeed. I can think of no greater joy. Edmund – Lord Partridge, I mean – will be back from his walk soon. You will of course wait to pay him your respects, Miss Braun?'

'It would be my pleasure, Lady Partridge,' Marianne replied sweetly.

Lady Partridge waved them both off with a flourish of her hand.

'Thank you, Lady Partridge – truly, thank you,' Lydia said as they headed out of the door, her heart still thumping.

She could stay – for now.

'Now, Miss Marmalade, let us go to the piano – we must start rehearsing immediately!' Marianne took Lydia's arm and walked her towards the large music room.

She sat at the piano and started to play the familiar carol and Lydia did her best to sing it as she had known it, played in the village hall in Hopperton by Mrs Didcot who couldn't really play with both hands and was known to fall asleep during a long tune. Lydia remembered that – despite others' complaints – whatever song she had been singing, her mum loved to hear her sing. She pictured her, smiling back at her with pride.

Lydia was almost enjoying herself when Bel leapt from her pocket and jumped on to the piano keys, landing on middle C, then jumped down on to the piano seat next to Marianne.

Lydia stopped, in a **panic**. Why was Bel deliberately risking being seen? Harriet's warning about sprites being mischievous came back to her and Lydia silently implored Bel not to move.

Marianne, who had been lost in the tune and playing with her eyes closed, now opened them. 'Did you hear that odd note, Lydia?' She looked utterly bemused.

'Hmm, no, I don't think I did hear anything that sounded strange or that shouldn't be there.'

Marianne shook her head, puzzled. 'I must be tired from all the playing. And here I am not offering you any practice at all, Lydia. Perhaps you shall play and

I can sing for a time!' She rose and gestured to Lydia to sit down.

Bel waved at Lydia and then **waggled** her bum at her. Lydia gulped. She could only play from memory rather than reading music and she did not know this carol at all. Marianne had risked so much to help her; Lydia was afraid she would regret her kindness once she learnt how far away from being a proper lady Lydia really was.

It's easy to forget that in these times, to be a proper lady you had to sing and sew and not be too loud. No one was very pleased if you had a brain, or were funny, or knew how to make a fart noise with your hand – which nowadays is what makes anyone 'proper' fun (sorry, not *proper*, in the old sense).

Lydia was **frantically** trying to think her way out of this particular pickle when Edmund entered the room. She let out a squeak of relief. 'EDMUND'S HERE!' she shouted.

He looked a little taken aback. 'I'm sorry to keep you waiting, Miss Braun, forgive me. I came as soon as Ronalds informed me you were here. What a lovely surprise!' He flushed on both his cheeks and ears and Lydia thought he looked more like a beetroot than the young Lord of Peppomberley.

'Not at all, Miss Marmalade has been excellent company.'

'Lydia! You are still here?'

Lydia nodded awkwardly, wondering if he disapproved of her as much as his mother did, but she was distracted by a **flash** of sparks from under the sofa. *Bel.*

'Miss Marmalade was about to play a tune. Perhaps we could take a turn about the room while she does so?' Marianne smiled at Edmund.

His cheeks **flushed** red and Lydia wondered quite what it was that made Marianne so keen on him. She was so clever and kind, and lovely. And he seemed so awkward and disapproving.

'Super! Yes, super! Thank you, Miss Marmalade.'

He offered Marianne his arm, looking at Lydia expectantly. There was no way out. She sat down and began to play 'Robin Adair'. Her mother had taught it to her, and she knew she could play it without stopping for at least one turn about the room. Although she really was a terrible piano player. She had barely practised, since they hadn't owned one at home.

But their interest in each other appeared to exceed the terrible accompaniment. Lydia noticed that when Marianne talked to Edmund she seemed less like a perfect vision of ladylike goodness, and more like an ordinary person who enjoyed laughing at what Edmund was saying. She couldn't really imagine Edmund being charming or funny, but he did seem rather more pleasant now. Neither of them resembled either of the people she had met at the awful dinner last night.

Lydia felt a sudden heat on her face and glanced up from her playing. Sitting on top of the music book was Bel. Her skirt was **sparking**, and Lydia could see it was starting to burn a hole in the papers.

'Bel!' she hissed. 'Come down from there! I thought your magic wasn't working!'

'It isn't! Not proper-like. But you can't deny it's nice to have fresh walnuts.' She glanced across the room. 'I have no idea how I am to get my real magic back with these two silly doves cooing about!'

'They are not silly doves! You're burning the music!'

Bel folded her arms. 'Lydia, you did wish me here and now you are leaving me about like a rotten redcurrant who is souring your pie!'

'I know and I'm sorry, Bel, but I am to behave as a polite young lady should, and right now I need to play the piano until they finish whatever it is they are doing walking round and round the room!'

'Conker and canker soup! Let's hurry them up then!' hissed Bel.

Bel fluttered down on to the piano keys. She began to jump, hop and cartwheel across the keys, making Lydia's playing sound, well, worse than it already did, and the tempo too fast. Lydia could only watch and listen in **horror**.

'Are you well, Lydia?' Marianne enquired, walking towards the piano. Edmund trailed behind her, frowning at Lydia.

Bel hopped back on to Lydia's lap and into her pocket.

'Yes, that is how I like to play sometimes. I often find the music too … restrictive,' she said with confidence.

'How charming you are, Miss Marmalade!' said Marianne. 'Well, I must return to my mother, but I do look forward to seeing you both at our Midwinter Ball.'

'The day shall not come soon enough,' Edmund said.

They stared at each other for an odd amount of time, until Lydia felt she should say something. 'I can't wait, Marianne!'

Edmund took Marianne's arm and led her out of the room.

Lydia realised she was finally alone. She wanted to run towards the kitchen but settled on a fast walk; she couldn't risk any more unladylike behaviour. She headed downstairs, opened the door to the kitchen and felt calmer, breathing in the smell of freshly baked bread mingled with the muffins Harriet was taking out of the oven.

'Miss Lyddy!' Harriet cried.

Lydia froze. The only other person who had ever called her Lyddy was her mum. She thought for a moment and then, somewhere inside, she decided it was nice to hear her nickname again.

'Oh, someone will be pleased to see—'

Before Harriet could finish her sentence a flash of brown jumped into Lydia's arms and licked her nose.

Lydia held him tightly, breathing in his biscuity doggy goodness. She glanced at his new bed. Harriet had found an old wicker basket and lined it with his blanket, near the warm stove. 'Oh, Collipop! I have missed you so much, but I see Harriet has taken good care of you!'

'Care! Miss Lyddy, he's nearly eaten me out of food this morning! Three drop-cakes, one egg, toast with marmalade, then, before I knew it, he got a carrot out of the pantry for a nibble too.' Colin looked a little guilty but very pleased with himself.

Lydia hugged him again. 'Oh, thank you, Harriet! I knew he would be safe with you.'

Harriet flushed a little. 'It's my pleasure, miss.' She paused to sniff and then wrinkled her nose. 'I smell burning; it's not those muffins, is it? No, they're already out.' Harriet looked confused, but Lydia knew what was happening. She patted her pocket and found it empty. Where was Bel now? She anxiously scanned the kitchen and saw a trail of yellow sparks hanging in the air, heading out of the back door.

'Harriet, may I take Colin outside? We might go and see Bertie.'

'Good idea! I've got more baking to do today. Just in case today's the day for the special announcement!' Harriet gave her a wink. 'Edmund and Marianne are sure to be engaged before Christmas. We all hope so anyway, so Lady P don't fly into a rage at her plans not working out.'

'Oh,' said Lydia. Of course – Lady Partridge wanted Marianne and Edmund to wed. And maybe they wanted that too. It would certainly make sense of the strange way they were looking at each other.

'We've all been on tenterhooks!' continued Harriet. 'Lady Braun is very rich indeed and there was some worry she would not approve of the match! But Edmund has charmed her so.'

'Does it matter that she is rich?' asked Lydia.

Harriet gave her a kind look, 'I wish it didn't, my duck. But folks like Lady P, they don't marry people for love, they marry for money and houses and titles. That's how they all stay so rich! Lady Braun hasn't been wealthy for long, in fact there's some who would look down on them for not being real gentry – but beggars can't be choosers. The Partridges are wealthy enough, but Peppomberley is a big estate and they need to keep marrying well to live the way they are accustomed to. Money marries money. So Lady Braun buys her way into an old family, and gets an invitation into high society, and they all get what they want, I suppose. Though I'd rather have a good night's sleep and some hot milk!' Harriet started kneading more dough, humming to herself.

Lydia was again confused by the bizarre ways of Peppomberley. What if Marianne *wanted* to marry someone poor? Would she be allowed? At least she seemed to like Edmund, despite him seeming quite dull.

In any case, Lydia had other things to worry about – she needed to find Bel. Where was she? They had some investigating to do.

All she knew was that the cheeky sprite had gone outside. Lydia placed Colin on the floor, wrapped her shawl around her and stepped out into the cold.

Chapter Nine
SEARCHING

Lydia **tramped** past the vegetable garden then marched through the formal gardens (keeping one eye out for any exciting-looking climbing trees). She looked back at the grand house and saw it did not look so large from this view. Or perhaps she was just getting used to it? She followed the gravel path a little further and then **paused** by a giant fountain that had been emptied for winter. There, atop the bit where the water would normally flourish out, some yellow sparks were sadly sputtering.

'Belamina!' Lydia shouted in her best cross voice. **'Come back down here now!'**

Bel jumped so much at the sound of her own name she fell off the spindly perch and bumped down on to the empty fountain floor.

'Blastering blackberries! I shall give you a fox tail if you make me jump like that again! Just as soon as I get my magic back, you wait, you'll have two tails, three tails, ten tails! And you'll never sit down comfy again and rich folks shall try and hunt you all season!'

'Bel! I'm sorry, but you can't wander off like that. If someone sees you—'

'I'll turn them into a toad with a huge, long tongue that doesn't fit in their mouth and they'll have to buy a bag to carry it round in!'

'You won't if you don't have any magic!' said Lydia. Bel pouted, scrambled up the edge of the empty pond and slumped on to Lydia's lap. Lydia felt the warmth from her skirt but noticed that it didn't seem as hot as it had done previously. The colour had faded to a paler orange.

'Bel, I need you to help me, not cause more mischief!' Lydia said.

'But the big feathery lady said you could stay?'

'Yes, but we need to solve the mystery of how she knows my mum, that's the only way I can see that might make the wish feel true. I don't even know why my mum sent me here.'

Bel **munched** on an acorn she'd found and put the acorn cup on her head as a hat. 'What we need is a plan. Where would Lady Partridge keep all her secrets? I bet her big ol' desk has got a lot of clues in it that could help us!'

'How could we ever look in it, Bel? She's always sat at it writing!'

'She goes to the toilet like everyone else! Must be

a few minutes she's not sat on her bum guarding her desk!' said Bel.

Lydia **giggled**, but she also felt a glimmer of hope. Bel was right – and maybe she would start being helpful, rather than causing trouble. The desk might hold a letter from her mother, or some other clue that would explain everything. But if Lydia was caught in there, she'd be sent away for sure.

A voice punctured her thoughts.

'Eh-oh!'

Lydia turned and could see a hand waving from the stables. Her heart lifted as she waved back to him. *Bertie might be able to help*, she thought. But she'd have to explain Bel to him first.

'Come on, Bel, there's someone I need you to meet.' She gently lifted Bel up to her shoulder, where she grabbed on to Lydia's shawl, **moaning** about how fast she was walking.

Colin ran into the stables first and found Bertie

deep in conversation with two beautiful grey horses. Colin **jumped** up at Bertie and the horses raised their legs and began to **stamp** their big, hoofed feet.

'All right, Mabel, all right, Merlin! It's only a little dog,' Bertie soothed. 'Don't mind them, Colin, they don't like being surprised.'

'Sorry, Bertie!' Lydia exclaimed. The horses' heads both turned at exactly the same time and stared right at Bel. The sprite dived into a hay bale. Lydia gasped.

'You all right there, miss?' Bertie laughed.

'Yes, thanks. You can call me Lydia, if you like. What … what lovely hay, is it yours?' Lydia patted it awkwardly.

'Well, belongs to the horses really.' Bertie raised his eyebrow and couldn't hide his smile. He carried on adjusting Mabel's saddle with well-practised ease.

Lydia glanced around for the sprite. How could she tell Bertie about Bel if she couldn't show him?

'Have you lived here all your life, Bertie?' Lydia asked, buying some time.

'Yes, Miss Lydia. My ma lives in a cottage not far from here, on land owned by the former Lord Partridge, before he passed. But I started working here when I was very young.'

Lydia took a breath. There was no sign of Bel. She would have to explain to Bertie and hope he understood. 'Bertie … there's someone I wanted you to meet—'

'Lawks!' Bertie interrupted, grabbing Lydia by the wrists and **leaping** in front of her. Smoke was rising out from the hay where she had been standing! Bertie grabbed a bucket of water from beside Mabel and chucked the entire thing over the smoking hay.

Lydia was desperately searching for Bel, hoping she was all right after her soaking.

'I've never seen anything like that in all my days. A hay bale in winter just set itself on fire!' Bertie was dumbfounded.

'I think I might know why it happened, Bertie ...'

'And something caught my eye as it started smoking. It was all these yellow sparks. Why, it looked as if a—' Bertie paused and looked at Lydia, embarrassed.

She searched Bertie's eyes, trying to decide how to answer. Could she trust him? She thought about how gentle he was with his horses. Surely he would never hurt a living thing. And Harriet was his aunt, so he must know about winter sprites. But would he believe her?

Lydia **burst** out, 'It was a sprite, Bertie. Her name is Bel and she's really good at getting into all sorts of mischief. You have to swear not to tell anyone, though!'

'A winter sprite! That's what I thought, Miss Lydia, but I was sore afraid you'd laugh at me if I said it out loud. Don't you worry, I won't tell a soul about it.'

He looked at her solemnly and Lydia knew she

had been right to trust him.

'But where's she gone? I gave her a soaking, she'll be frozen solid if we don't get her dry.'

At that moment, Lydia heard a sneeze from inside the bale. And there was Bel, soaking wet, her red hair stuck to her face, looking very, very cross.

'Well nice to meet you too, Mr Bertie Bumpkin, throwing water at me as if I was a pond sprite!'

'So sorry, Bel! I hope you can forgive me, it's a real honour to meet a proper sprite.' Bertie bent to shake her tiny hand, and smiled at her. Bel humphed, but gave him a little grin back and Lydia could tell she liked him.

Just then they heard a gruff voice nearby, shouting at another servant.

'Ronalds!' they whispered.

'I'd better leave, Bertie!' muttered Lydia. 'I'll see you soon!'

Lydia grabbed Bel and a shower of yellow sparks tumbled off her damp wings.

Bertie watched them both dart away. He shook his head: things at Peppomberley had certainly livened up since Lydia arrived.

***

Lydia ran back towards the house. A light drizzle started to fall as Bel wiggled and kicked in her hand.

'Put me down! I don't need to be carried like a froglet moving ponds!'

'Well, stop flying off then!' snapped Lydia.

'I am looking for clues to solve this mystery! If we can't find out more about your mum and Lady Partridge and make you feel as if she is here with you, then your wish-tastrophe won't ever get granted and I'll be stuck here without any magic,' Bel huffed. 'I want to get home, you know! Anyway, I can't fly anywhere until my wings have dried out. Oh, I am *wretched indeed*! Most unhappy!'

Lydia stopped and lifted the sprite up to her face. She really did look a sight. Her hair was damp now and some hay was still sticking to her skirt. She smelt like a put-out fire.

'Unhappy?' Lydia was a little confused. It was she who was in trouble, on thin ice, sent far away from home. 'What do you have to be unhappy about? So you can't get home for a while, it's not the end of the world!' She heard the edge to her voice but she couldn't stop it.

'Oh, my hedges and broom sweeps. You are a rotten egg sometimes, Lydia Marmalade.' Bel folded her arms and glared at her. 'I had a life, you know, before you made a stupid wish for something impossible—'

'It wasn't stupid!' Lydia **shouted** in frustration. She wanted to scream and tell Bel she couldn't possibly understand how much she missed her mum, how in that moment she'd wanted to believe with all her heart that she might see her again. How could anyone understand how she felt? But her heart softened as she looked at the little sprite, who was now refusing to look at Lydia – as much as was possible given she was in her hand. Lydia had been sent to Peppomberley with no choice and now Bel was trapped there too, and although an accident, it was Lydia's fault.

'Bel, I'm sorry, I—'

Before she could say more Lady Partridge and Lady Braun appeared at the top of the entrance steps. Lady Braun was hopping down the stairs and saying something to Lady Partridge, who was nodding and smiling. Lydia saw the Brauns' pretty carriage waiting at the foot of the stairs, and there was Marianne sitting inside.

Lydia realised this was her chance to search Lady Partridge's desk, while she was occupied outside. 'Sorry again!' she whispered, gently placing Bel into her pocket and pinching the sides together so she couldn't get back out.

She had to walk past the carriage to get to the house. 'Hello, Marianne!' she called cheerfully and went to walk on by, but Marianne's face was blotchy and her eyes were red, as though she'd been crying. 'Are you well, Marianne?' she asked kindly.

Her friend's eyes filled with tears, and she looked for a moment as if she would say something, but she shook her head. 'Nothing, Lydia, 'tis nothing. I am quite well.' She smiled weakly.

Lady Braun appeared suddenly, 'Ah, Miss Marmalade! You have heard the good news from Marianne! She is indeed engaged to the fine young Lord Partridge himself!'

Lydia looked at Marianne, who turned away from her mother.

'Congratulations, Lady Braun! And you, Marianne.' Lydia tried to smile at her, but Marianne would not meet her eye. Perhaps she was worried that Edmund only wanted her money! Lydia felt awful for her friend. She wished she could speak to Marianne alone.

'We shall announce the engagement forthwith!' Lady Braun hauled herself into the carriage as her servant closed the door behind her. Colin and Lydia took a step back as it rode off, the horses kicking up dust as they headed past the forest road.

Lady Partridge re-entered the house without acknowledging Lydia, no doubt headed straight back to her drawing room. The search would have to wait. At least she hadn't seemed to notice that Colin was outside the kitchen.

The Brauns' carriage disappeared from view, and Lydia felt a sharp kick from her pocket. Bel! 'I'll let you out soon, I promise!'

Lydia thought again of how sad Marianne had looked. Even though she had money and a home and a mum, she still wasn't happy.

Lydia sighed heavily and Colin gave a yip.

'You're right, Colin, nothing makes less sense than other people.'

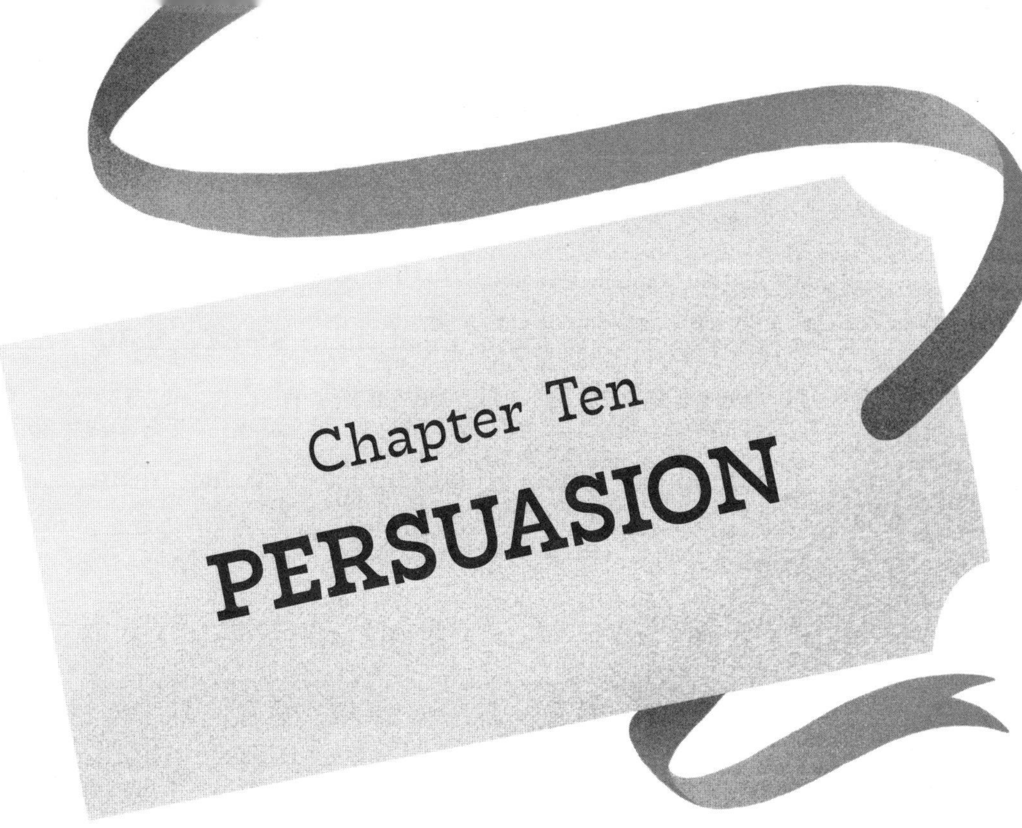

Chapter Ten
PERSUASION

A week had passed since Edmund and Marianne's engagement had been announced. Peppomberley had been filled with much activity. The wedding date had been set by Lady Partridge and Lady Braun for the new year; Edmund seemed excited and yet also apprehensive – he could often be found at the front door asking Ronalds if Marianne had left a card or called for him, but she hadn't visited since the proposal took place.

Lydia, Bel and Bertie hadn't had many spare moments, but they'd spent all of them **searching** for clues. There must be something in Peppomberley that would make Lydia feel connected to her mum again, and make the wish feel true. They'd explored as many rooms as they could, Lydia wondering at how many and how empty most of them were. They'd come across one huge pair of locked double doors, and when Bel squeezed through the keyhole she reported a 'huge massive whopper of a room'. Lydia had also discovered that Bel was right – if she got too far away from her, she'd feel an **uncomfortable** pulling sensation.

On one occasion, they'd finally found Lady Partridge's drawing room unoccupied. While Bertie kept watch at the door, Lydia and Bel had carefully searched her desk, Colin sniffing at their heels. Lydia found a stuck drawer at the bottom that rattled when she shook it, and Bel was just about to try some magic when—

'Watch out!' hissed Bertie. 'Ronalds about!'

Bel hid in a quill pot while Bertie ran to the window and made a leap into the flowerbed outside. Lydia gave one more tug at the drawer and out it popped, shooting out a dusty old dog's collar into her hands. Hastily closing the drawer, she hid the collar behind her back and pretended to be studying a painting of some grumpy-looking children.

'What on earth are you doing in Lady Partridge's drawing room?' scoffed Ronalds, striding in. 'Don't you have a tree to fall out of?'

But Lydia paid him no heed. She was too busy thinking about the dog collar. As she headed out into the corridor, she examined it. It looked as if it was for a very small dog, a long time ago – but the name lovingly sewn on to it was ... *Colin.*

This was a **mystery** indeed, and Lydia couldn't work out how to solve it. Had Lady Partridge too had a dog called Colin? Surely not. Lady Partridge clearly hated dogs. She couldn't **wait** to talk to Bel and Bertie about this strange new development.

***

Meanwhile, wedding preparations were underway. Lady Partridge had an opinion on how every little single thing should be done just so – the 'Partridge way', as she often referred to it. She needed a new dress, new gloves, hat, reticule bag, shoes, feathers that matched the ribbon that matched the brooch – Lydia was quite sure Lady Partridge would look like a blackberry, dressed in so many shades of purple.

The wedding was so distracting to Lady Partridge, she did not notice if Lydia dined with them or not, and so Lydia had even managed to have supper with Harriet and Bertie in the kitchen, Colin curled up on her toes to keep them warm, just as he had done in

Hopperton. Dinner in the kitchen was different from upstairs. There were the leftovers from the upstairs meal, plus huge meaty pies with thick crusts, and glorious gooey puddings. Harriet would let you take a huge portion and wouldn't fuss about mess either. Everyone's places were covered in crumbs and stains and nobody minded a fig, as Harriet would say.

Ronalds had also been so **busy** with all of Lady Partridge's requests that he had barely had any time to shout at Lydia when he did catch sight of her. But she had learnt to avoid him by not crossing the main hall after breakfast and to make sure she left the kitchen before he came for his cake and tea in the afternoons.

Peppomberley was still too large, too creaky, too full of hidden corners, but Lydia had started to find her way around. She'd found a few good climbing trees in the grounds, although Martha was always telling her that *proper ladies* didn't have grazed knees and muddy skirts.

While Lydia was **settling** into life at Peppomberley, the last week had been tough for Bel. Despite their dedicated search, and the **mysterious** dog collar, they still hadn't found any more clues as to how Lady Partridge and Lydia's mum were connected and, as each day passed, Bel became more and more homesick. She had taken to staring out the window, only talking to Lydia to tell her what birds were stealing berries or who looked like they had fallen out with the badgers.

On one particular morning Bel didn't want to go anywhere with Lydia. She stayed staring at the woods so long, that Lydia went to find her some branches and a piece of soft woollen blanket to line it with, and made her a sort of nest on the windowsill to remind her of home. Lydia noticed that the flames on Bel's skirt had faded even more, which couldn't be a good sign, but she was afraid to ask about it and upset the sprite further. It felt as though time was running out.

She tried to appeal to Bel, to pull her out of her mood. 'Bel! You are a winter sprite! You spread warmth and magic when animals and people need it most. We will solve this wish if we keep trying! You can't give up!'

'Can't I? You should have seen the winter sprites in the Sprite Olympics, we gave up after one round of ice skating because we were too cold.'

'I'm sure that's not true.'

'No point racing against ice sprites,' Bel said moodily and **slumped** back into her nest before curling into a ball. But Lydia had an idea. Tomorrow was the Midwinter Ball. There would be people there who knew Lady Partridge and may have even known her mother. Surely they could find more **clues** about why Lydia had been sent to Peppomberley – a link that, once discovered, would grant the wish and free Bel.

Lady Partridge had tried several times to dissuade

Lydia from going, but when a dress from Marianne arrived with a note personally expressing how much she wanted Lydia to attend, she had to **reluctantly** agree. Lydia knew that if she put even one toe wrong whilst at the ball there would certainly be trouble with a big T. She had to be on her very, very, very best behaviour. She knew she could do that, but keeping Bel in check would be a **trickier** matter.

Chapter Eleven
THE MIDWINTER BALL

On the afternoon of the ball, Martha entered Lydia's room with a bowl of water, a towel, a hairbrush, many hair pins and a resolute look on her face.

'This won't be quick, Miss Marmalade,' she said as she came in and Lydia had nodded. Lydia hated having her hair brushed, but she had to get to the ball, so she needed to look like she was meant to be there.

Martha brushed and pulled and muttered to herself and then stomped out of the room for a bit shouting,

'This hair is impossible!' before coming back in to tackle and plait and pull Lydia's bushy brown hair finally into neatness. Eventually she stood back and marvelled at her handiwork. 'You look better than I thought you were going to,' Martha said triumphantly.

Lydia tried to deny it but she was excited. She had never been to a real ball before; Hopperton had nothing as fancy as that. She was looking forward to seeing the Brauns' grand house – and Harriet said she thought there might be pineapples to look at and maybe even try!

Martha returned with Marianne's old dress. Lydia **gasped** as Martha held it up to her. It was a beautiful burnt orange colour. There was a golden ribbon around the edges of it and tiny stars were sewn all along the hem.

Martha helped Lydia step into it and buttoned her up, then led her to the looking glass. Lydia made a small **squeaking** noise when she saw herself.

Martha smiled. 'I didn't think you could look this fine, Miss Marmalade!'

'Thank you, Martha!' Lydia laughed. 'Neither did I!' It felt strange to see herself look like, well, a lady – like a neat, tidy sister she had never met before. She didn't like how long it had taken to look like this, but she didn't hate the end result either. She wished her mum could see her in this dress. She wouldn't ever have believed Lydia was going to an actual ball. It would have made her so happy.

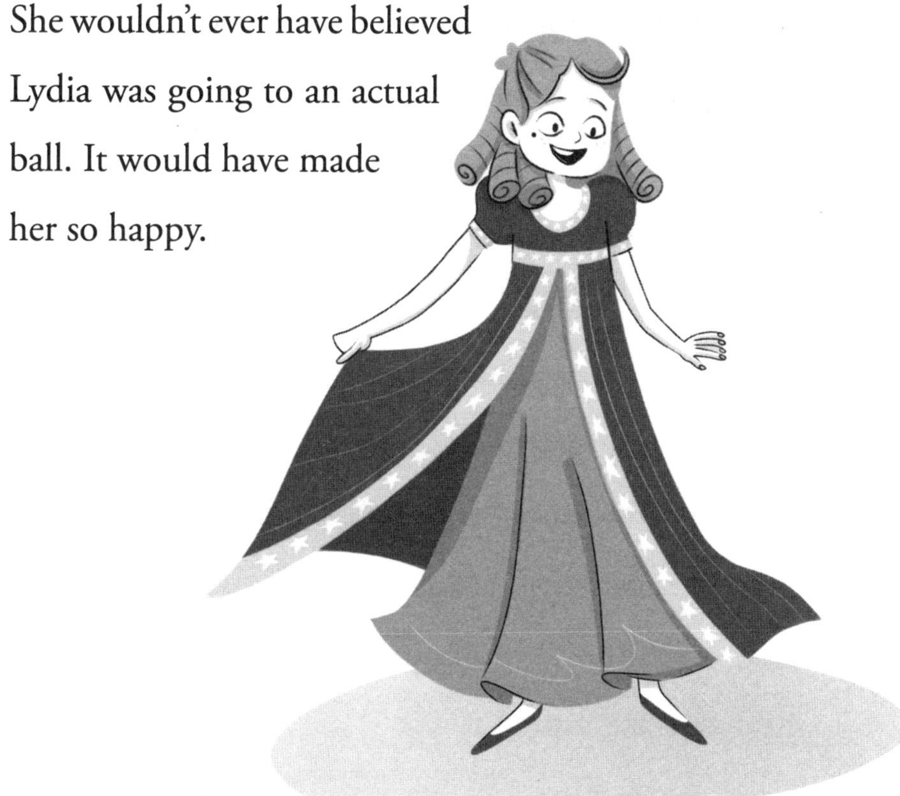

There was a shriek from far away that was unmistakeably Lady Partridge. 'Oh my, she must need help with her feathers. I'll be back soon, Miss Marmalade. Don't sit down and crease your dress, or lie down, or … just don't move!' Martha shouted as she bolted out of the door.

Lydia checked on Bel, who was still sleeping in her twig nest. Just then there was a loud bang from downstairs. Maybe Lady Partridge had thrown something in a fit of rage? Bel woke with a start.

'Oh! Broomsticks, are we going now?' she asked, jumping out of the branches and shaking herself off.

'Bel,' said Lydia, summoning her serious voice. 'Tonight is very important. As well as trying to find out anything about my mum, I have to behave as a proper lady should. Lady Partridge will certainly send me away if I mess up again. And then you'll have to come with me and you'll never get home. We cannot make more trouble.'

'Trouble! Toadstools and frog's legs! Me, do something troublesome?' Bel clasped her hand to her chest in mock disbelief.

Lydia gave her a strong look.

'All right, I really and truly promise to behave. I cannot stay here like a goose waiting to be cooked!'

Marianne had sent the perfect dress, but it had no pockets. Lydia rooted amongst her things and found her faded reticule.

'You'll have to get in this, Bel. We'll be in the carriage with Lady Partridge and Edmund.'

Bel folded her arms and stamped her foot. 'Well, in all my life as a winter sprite never have I been shoved away in as many things as I have this last week, as though I was a bad smell! Outrageous!' She stuck her nose in the air defiantly. 'You're to get me out twice at the party so I can see things. Stanley will be so jealous that I've been to a ball!'

'Maybe just once ...' Lydia suggested.

'Twice, or I'll burn a hole through this bag!'

'Fine, twice, but only when it's safe!'

Lydia took the soft wool from her twig nest and lined the bag with it. She took a walnut from the jar she kept by her bed for Bel (they were still working their way through them) and placed it in there too. Bel hopped on to her hand and Lydia carefully placed her inside. Just as she pulled the string on the bag, Martha rat-a-tatted the door.

'You best come now Miss Marmalade, Lady Partridge is leaving and saying she will go without you!'

Lydia ran down the corridor and dived down the huge staircase. Lady Partridge was standing at the front door looking annoyed.

She turned and took Lydia in, from top to toe. 'You've worked marvels with her hair, Martha, I never suspected it could look like that. And the dress is, of course, very suitable and becoming. Marianne is a girl of taste. Those shoes are *very* gold. But' – she gestured at Lydia's bag – 'that is in need of mending. Leave it here.'

'Oh no, you see I need a bag—'

'What on earth could you need to carry, child?' snapped Lady Partridge, peacock feathers wiggling jauntily in her hat.

Lydia felt her throat tense. She twisted the bag's cotton tie handles in her hands. 'But—'

'Miss Marmalade. Leave that bag,' Lady Partridge said firmly. Lydia recognised her final tone. She placed the bag on a chair by the side of the front door. She opened it and saw Bel's furious face, and pulled it shut again. Ronalds appeared.

'Young Lord Partridge has ridden on ahead, ma'am.'

'Impatient boy! We shall ride in the carriage, Ronalds, quick smart!'

As Lady Partridge began to descend the grand stairs, Lydia took a moment to whisper to Bel, 'I don't know what to do! I can't bring the bag but where on earth can I hide you?'

Bel was fuming. Her skirt had even gained a little colour back. 'Well, if that silly feathery lady thinks she tells me, a *sprite*, where I can and cannot go, she's in for a lesson on magic.'

'Bel, what are you going to—' Before Lydia could finish, Bel **clenched** her fists, bent her knees, flew into the air and lowered herself on to Lady Partridge's hat, nestling down amongst the enormous feathers. If Bel was connected to Lydia, Lydia was now connected to Lady Partridge, which was going to make finding out clues all the more difficult. Lydia placed her palm against her forehead. **Sprites!**

She ran down the grand stone stairs and stopped at the door to the carriage. Lady Partridge was already settling herself and her many layers of taffeta into the seat. It was then Lydia saw Bertie, who had been preparing the horses. He was dressed in a smart uniform, matching the coach driver and the other footmen, who were already seated and holding the reins of Mabel and Merlin.

Bertie was staring at Lady Partridge, open-mouthed. When he saw Lydia he said meaningfully, 'Miss Lydia, I think a someone, a some*thing* might be on top of—'

'Come now, Miss Marmalade! We haven't all night!' Lady Partridge tutted with annoyance from inside the carriage.

Lydia gave Bertie a pained look and **hurriedly** climbed inside.

They made their way through the forest towards the Brauns' house. As they jiggled down the bumpy country lanes, Lydia could see Bel rolling around and occasionally clinging on to a feather to steady herself. She seemed to be having the time of her life.

It wasn't the safest or most secure hiding place for Bel, but there was nothing to be done now. They just had to get through the ball without anyone else seeing her. And hope Bel stayed hidden.

Suddenly, Lady Partridge turned to Lydia. 'This is a *very* important evening for my family, Miss Marmalade. I want to see *perfect* behaviour from you. *No* chatting to the servants, *no* making a spectacle of yourself and *no* trouble.'

'Yes, Lady Partridge.'

'I understand you should want to come to such a grand event, Miss Marmalade. I was apprehensive as to whether you would fit in, in such *elegant* surroundings. But I do not wish to deny you any enjoyment, I am sure you have never had much before, living as you did.'

Lydia paused, trying to untangle what Lady Partridge had said to work out if it had been nice or not.

'I am excited to go to the ball, Lady Partridge. Although please don't think I never had fun in

Hopperton.' Lydia was unsure why she'd said this and risk **irritating** Lady Partridge, but something inside her wanted to defend her past and the memories she held there.

'Indeed, child? I am surprised. You had so little in terms of entertainment, just your neighbours in that ridiculously small village.'

'Yes, it's true that Hopperton is small – but full of the friendliest people I ever met. The kindest too. There was always so much laughter.' Lydia got caught in a memory and smiled.

Lady Partridge looked at her. 'But Catherine—' She stopped herself.

'Yes? My mother? You knew each other before I was born, I believe, Lady Partridge?' Lydia held her breath in anticipation.

Lady Partridge **gazed** out of the window at the darkening sky. 'No, we did not know each other, Miss Marmalade. We were distant, very distant cousins, by marriage, I believe. I never met her.'

Lydia wanted to ask more questions, but they had arrived and the carriage came to a stop.

They pulled up to the front of the Brauns' country manor. It was large, though not quite so grand as Peppomberley. As if reading her mind, Lady Partridge said, 'This is their *country* residence, Miss Marmalade.'

Lydia nodded, trying not to show her shock at someone having more than one house. What on earth did they fill it with? *You'd have to buy two of everything*, she thought. She could imagine her mother complaining that it would only be double the cleaning, before she realised the Brauns probably didn't do the sweeping themselves.

Lady Partridge was helped out of the carriage by a footman, hauling herself and her grand outfit out of the small door. Lydia could see Bel clinging on to the hat as she juddered down the steps. She followed and they walked up to the house and heard the beautiful music coming from inside. Two smartly dressed footmen, wearing ornate jackets, opened the doors – and there stood Marianne. She was flushed, but she looked as charming as ever. Her hair was perfectly piled on to her head and she wore the most beautiful and delicate pink dress along with her exquisite ruby necklace. Edmund appeared behind her.

'Ah Lydia, you are here!' Marianne greeted her. 'See I have not worn white, for I knew you were coming!' She laughed, and Lydia felt like she was with the big sister she had never had. Marianne ushered them in, and they passed through a grand hall bedecked with greenery. Everywhere you looked there were candles and decorations, sweet treats piled on to tables, and finely dressed guests.

Lady Partridge **wrinkled** her nose at it all. 'People do go overboard these days,' she said to herself. There was a roaring log fire, which Lady Partridge immediately sat herself down next to. Lydia stood next to her, **clasping** her hands in front of her and trying to look ladylike, but Marianne insisted she show her the ballroom and they walked to the other side of the hall through two huge open doors. A string quartet echoed around the whole room. In the middle people were dancing in such fine clothes, Lydia couldn't tear her eyes from them. It was the finest party Lydia had ever seen.

'What's that?' she enquired. A **large** green fir tree stood at the back of the hall, looking like it had been dragged in from a real-life forest.

'Oh, 'tis Mama and Papa's tradition,' Marianne explained. 'My family are from Germany, where people bring in not just a Yule log but a Yule tree – a Christmas tree if you will – and decorate it to celebrate the winter season.'

The tree was **covered** in small candles and swathed with red ribbon and Lydia **marvelled** at it. Then Edmund took Marianne's hand, and they headed to the dance floor. And suddenly, Lydia was unaccompanied at a ball, which was not very ladylike. She must get back to Lady Partridge and Bel – the last thing she needed was Bel jumping out of her feathery hiding place.

But Lydia couldn't help but stay a moment longer.

Her mother would have loved this – the beautiful dresses, the music, the dancing. Although she would have hated the hats. '*Feathers are for birds, Lyddy, they look far sillier on us!*' Lydia was grateful to still hear her voice in her head.

A bittersweet sadness over took her and she turned to the tree. It was tall and grand, and smelt of the woods. Lydia leant in and gave a great big sniff of its branches. Through the window, she could see tiny snowflakes starting to fall on the grounds outside.

The whirling and turning couples were gliding across the floor. The ladies would swirl into the middle every now and then and take another hand before they all turned round and danced the other way. It looked more complicated than the country dances Lydia had seen at home, and more beautiful too. In the middle, Edmund and Marianne walked down the aisle of guests, hand in hand. The dance floor was full of congratulations for them, but Marianne looked sad again. She carried a soft white fan which she hid her face behind so the revellers could not see how little she was smiling.

Lydia **wished** she knew how to help Marianne feel better, but right now she needed to hurry back to Lady Partridge. She went over to the grand fire where Lady Partridge was sat, deep in conversation with two other ladies. Perhaps she'd forgotten Lydia was there – this was the perfect opportunity to eavesdrop. She stood behind a curtain so she could listen in for a moment.

'Why, Catherine was such a marvellous dancer, was she not, dear Lady Partridge?' said the taller lady, wearing a larger headpiece than Lydia believed a head could hold.

Catherine! Lydia froze to hear that name. Could they be talking about her mother? Lady Partridge simply gave a tight nod.

'Oh, the finest in the county!' the other lady exclaimed. 'Such a shame she—'

Lydia was leaning in so far to listen she **slipped** and fell out of her hiding place and fell in a heap behind them.

'May I help you, Lydia?' Lady Partridge snapped.

'Oh yes, I was just admiring your hat and the fine embroidery upon it.'

'There is no embroidery on my hat, child.'

'Oh.' Lydia stared at the hat some more. She also saw that there was no Bel on her hat either. 'Ah yes, indeed I was wrong. I must have been thinking of another hat.'

Lady Partridge **narrowed** her eyes.

Lydia needed to find Bel! 'Erm, may I go and admire the Christmas tree once again? It really is a wonder!'

Lady Partridge looked irked by the question, but smiled tightly. 'Of course, my dear. I shall come and find you in a moment.'

Lydia did her curtsey again, which elicited a puzzled look from one of the ladies. Lydia sighed.

She'd thought she'd got better at it!

She ran back into the ballroom, but she couldn't see Bel anywhere! Neither could she feel the pull between them, so Bel must be nearby.

As she was wondering whether to start searching everyone's heads, she suddenly saw an orange **flash** high up in the tree.

Lydia felt anger rising. Why didn't Bel listen to her? She had promised to behave, but instead had gone and done what she wanted, as usual. Lydia stopped in her tracks. Bel's behaviour reminded her of someone … herself.

Perhaps Bel didn't mean to disobey Lydia. It's just that these weren't the right rules for her.

Lydia **hissed** up to her, 'Bel! Bel! Come down here now!' Bel dived down further into the tree and hid amongst the spiky pines.

There was nothing for it. Lydia grabbed as much tree as she could and shook it, trying to be as quiet as possible. She could see Bel **swinging** around but although she was little, she was fierce, and she would not let go. She **glared** at Lydia and shouted down (in her small sprite voice), 'Frolicking frostbite! Stop waggling the tree, Lyddy, or I shall fall and crash on to my bottom!'

The two women Lady Partridge had been speaking to appeared by Lydia's side just as she shouted into the tree, **'Oh Bel, please come down!'**

'Is everything quite well, my dear?' one asked.

'Oh yes,' Lydia said quickly. 'Yes, why I am just … singing and shouting into the tree as we used to do in Hopperton. We need to let the tree know that if it doesn't listen to us, then spring will not come.' She stared at the tree with **gritted** teeth.

'So many strange rumours about this Hopperton,' the other lady whispered to her sister. 'Lady Partridge is indeed more kind than we knew to take in such a wild thing …'

Lydia's heart sank. She looked at her beautiful dress, now covered in pine needles, and she could feel her pretty hairstyle coming undone.

Bel stuck her tongue out at her and **disappeared** back into the tree. As Lydia gave it one last shake, one of the candles attached to a low branch fell over and began to burn, slowly at first and then, as the tree was so dried out, the flames moved faster. Lydia **screamed** and the guests near her stopped dancing and started to **panic** as they noticed the fire.

'Bel! Jump out, quickly!'

Bel looked at Lydia, her eyes wide with fear.

Suddenly there was a slap of water, as a huge wave hit the tree. Lydia turned to see Bertie holding a vase almost as big as he was, a pile of flowers at his feet. The fire was out! The guests **cheered**, apart from Lady Braun who, unfortunately, had made her way to the tree to see what the commotion was, and was now soaked in mucky old flower water.

Lydia ran to Bertie. 'Oh, well *done*!'

'I saw the fire from the window,' he whispered urgently. 'I watched Bel fly into the tree and was keeping an eye on her, but I didn't dare risk coming inside, only then I had to!'

Bel quickly stepped on to Lydia's open hands before anyone could notice her. She was **trembling**.

'Second time you soaked me, Bertie Boo!' she said, her teeth chattering.

Bertie took off his cap, Bel climbed inside, and he swiftly put it back on his head, just as Lady Partridge appeared behind Lydia.

'Lady Partridge!' Lady Braun was beside herself, her feathered headpiece stuck to one cheek and her ringlets now quite straight from the soaking she had received. 'Is this your boy? What is he doing in here? And Miss Marmalade! I see you are also part of this mischief!'

Lydia opened her mouth to explain but Lady

Partridge stepped forward and raised her hand to silence her. She didn't look cross or even embarrassed; she simply wouldn't look at Lydia. 'Miss Marmalade, to the carriage immediately.'

Lydia couldn't even defend herself. There would be no going back from this amount of trouble. This was Trouble. Doubled.

As Lydia turned to leave, there was a huge **cry** from the dance floor. Everyone turned to see who had made the dreadful noise. It was Marianne, crying, **'My necklace! My necklace! It's gone!'**

Lady Braun turned around to see Marianne clutching her neck, empty of its red jewel, and immediately fainted! Edmund managed to catch Lady Braun before she slipped to the floor. Someone quickly produced smelling salts and they were wafted under her nose. She awoke with a groan, sat upright and pointed at Bertie. 'It was him! I saw him peering through the window, then slipping into the room when we were distracted by the fire!'

Everyone turned to Bertie, who went bright red. 'Please, no, I—'

Lydia couldn't help herself. She burst out, 'That's not true! Bertie had nothing to do with it! Nothing at all!' The whole room stared at her in silence and disbelief.

'Marianne!' Lydia ran to her. 'You must know it wasn't Bertie. He's such a good person, why, he would never ever do anything like this!'

Marianne looked away, tears running down her face. Lydia was **furious**. This was more important than a necklace. Bertie's reputation was in danger. If he was thought a thief, he would lose his job and his home, perhaps Harriet would too. Lydia tried again, 'Marianne! Please! You must say something!'

Marianne stared at the floor. Edmund came to comfort her.

'Calm yourself, Miss Marmalade. Miss Marianne

is most distraught.' Lydia thought that he cast her a glance of sympathy as he led the pale and shaky Marianne away, but perhaps she'd imagined it.

The ball was beginning to recover from the drama, and the music began again.

Lady Partridge had taken Lady Braun aside and was speaking into her ear. She then strode over to Lydia and took her firmly by the hand. 'Enough! We are leaving. Bertie, follow me.'

Lydia tried to read Bertie's face, but he just looked scared. This was all her fault! Bertie had just been trying to help her and Bel.

Lady Partridge marched outside, ushered Lydia into the waiting carriage, and slammed the door shut. They rode home in silence.

Chapter Twelve
TO LISTEN AND LEARN

Back at Peppomberley, Lady Partridge told Lydia to go upstairs, then went into her drawing room. Lydia pretended to go up the stairs, but as soon as she heard Lady Partridge shut her door, she ran down to the kitchen to find Bertie.

As she came into the warm room, Harriet was setting down three different buns, a sandwich and a plate of biscuits in front of Bertie. To Lydia's horror, Ronalds was also there. Lydia could tell he was thoroughly enjoying the drama, despite Bertie being so terrified.

'Who knows, Master Herbert?' droned Ronalds. 'Depends how Lady Braun sees fit to punish you for such a terrible act of criminality. You might even be thrown into jail!'

Harriet let out a sob. 'Ronalds! You stop it right this instant, Bertie is a good lad and Lady Partridge knows it!'

Colin ran up to Lydia with **yips** of joy. She picked him up and came over to the large wooden table.

'Oh, Miss Lyddy! What a mess and a pickle! Surely, they know it was not Bertie who took that silly necklace!' Harriet pulled her in for a **huge** hug.

'Of course, Harriet, they know Bertie would never do anything like that!'

'But what was he doing inside the house? He knows better than that! He hasn't said a word to me since you got back!'

Lydia looked at Bertie, who glanced at her then at

his hat, which was sitting on the table. It moved ever so slightly, and she saw a small hand sneak out, take a crumb of cheese and quickly draw itself back in.

'It's all my fault, Harriet,' said Lydia quietly.

'Of course! Of course!' Ronalds was almost dancing with happiness now. 'I should have known Miss Marmalade was involved somehow. You see, Herbert, being friends with such a specimen as Miss Marmalade may not seem like such a good idea now, eh?' He cackled to himself and took a large bite of Bertie's bun.

Lydia nodded. Ronalds was right. Bertie was in trouble … because of her. Bel was stuck here … because of her. Lady Partridge must be regretting ever letting Lydia within sight of Peppomberley.

But Lydia was sure she could put one thing right at least. She couldn't let Bertie get **blamed** for this.

She felt an idea click into her head. She had to speak to Lady Partridge; she knew it wouldn't be easy, but she had to try. She stood up and grabbed Bertie's hat, whilst Ronalds was distracted stuffing his face with another bun. She marched out of the kitchen and into the servants' stairwell, opening Bertie's cap to find Bel had tucked herself into the band on the inside and was fast asleep. Lydia looked at Bel's skirt. It was still crackling quietly but with nothing like the heat from before. She was getting weaker. Lydia knew that even if she did solve Bertie's mess, there was another, bigger one, to solve next.

***

Lydia knocked carefully on the door to Lady Partridge's drawing room. She had changed back into her old dress and gently placed Bel into her pocket. The door was slightly open and she could hear another voice in the room. *Edmund.*

'What is it, Miss Marmalade?' Lady Partridge looked tired.

'I'm sorry, but I had to come and explain what really happened at the ball. There was a fire in the tree and Bertie ran in to put it out before anyone got hurt. He's a hero, not a thief! You can ask the other guests, too!'

Lady Partridge held up her hand. Lydia braced herself.

'Lydia, the accusation by Lady Braun is serious. If we say we believe Bertie, it would mean a lot of difficulties …' She glanced at Edmund. 'If we do not agree with Lady Braun, we are calling her a liar. Bertie should never have come inside the house and placed himself under suspicion. I have convinced Lady Braun to wait a few days before calling the constable, and hopefully the necklace will turn up. Now, this has been a long day and I think we should all go to bed.'

'All will be well, Miss Marmalade …' Edmund started. Then he looked at his toes and trailed off.

Lydia left the room. On the one hand, Lady Partridge clearly didn't believe Bertie was a thief. That counted for something. But until the jewel was found, he would still be in danger.

Lydia couldn't understand why Marianne had turned away from her at the ball. She'd thought they trusted each other, but maybe she was wrong. She knew nothing of these people really, or this world.

Lydia trudged up the stairs, her body aching with tiredness and disappointment. Tonight was supposed to be about solving the wish and setting Bel free, but they were no closer to the truth about her mother and now Bertie was at risk as well as Bel.

Before she climbed into bed, she looked out of her window and saw the deepening blanket of snow settling on the garden, quietening the outside world. She longed for someone to wrap her up right now and tell her everything was going to be all right. She remembered her mother's voice singing the lullaby she used to sing when Lydia was little, as if her voice was coming from far down a long corridor.

The west is always calling you
But you shall never know
That what the west is calling you for
Is a lesson takes time to show.

Chapter Thirteen
THE SEARCH

A few days had passed since the Midwinter Ball and, although life had thankfully been **quiet**, they were no closer to solving the mystery – and the necklace was still missing. She knew Bertie had had nothing to do with its **disappearance**, but who had?

Bel had also not been the same since the fire – she had taken to sleeping lots, which was making Lydia worry. She was always asleep when Lydia went to breakfast and at night when Lydia was drifting off, Bel would often be staring out of the window at the dark forest. Her skirt no longer crackled, and occasionally a puff of grey smoke drifted around her. She had picked up her wand a few times, but Lydia had seen not a single spark come off it and each time Bel had put it down, embarrassed.

Lydia had tried everything she could think of to cheer Bel up. She had sneaked dried fruits and other treats out of the kitchen, but Bel hardly ate anything.

That morning, Lydia was full of **determination**, and set off to the stables to find Bertie. The weather was the coldest it had been all winter, so Lydia wrapped Bel up snugly in her blanket and placed her into a small basket, which she hoped would be more comfortable for a sleep than a squashed pocket, and set out.

As she walked down the hard, frozen path, she thought about Marianne, who had not visited since the ball. She had been so warm when Lydia first met her, like a big sister, and now she seemed as distant as the far-off hills.

Lydia entered the stable and found Bertie talking to the horses as usual, making sure they were more contented than any of the humans who lived in Peppomberley.

'Bertie!' Lydia ran to him and placed Bel's basket carefully on a hay bale.

'She's not going to set it on fire again, is she, Miss Lydia?' Bertie joked.

'I doubt it.' Lydia looked down at the tiny sprite. 'What's wrong?'

'She isn't well! She keeps sleeping and her fire seems to be going out – and I don't know how to stop it. Maybe if we kept her warmer then—'

'Slow down! There are a hundred thoughts there and I've only two ears!'

'I wish we could do something!'

Bel gave an angry huff as Bertie lifted the blankets

off her. 'I've never seen a real sprite before,' he said. 'I still can't believe it's not a trick of the light. But you're right, she doesn't look like she did before.'

Bel **grabbed** the blankets back and **pulled** them over her head.

'Shivering snowflakes! I'm colder than an icicle having an ice cream whilst ice-skating!'

Bel peered back over the blanket.

'Oh, hello there, Bertie Boo!'

Lydia felt a wave of **relief** that Bel was awake and seemed to have some of her usual attitude back again.

Bel looked down at her skirts and sighed. 'That water near extinguished me. I'm not much of a warming winter sprite these days – I'm turning into a smoke siren and they are the WORST.'

'A smoke siren? Are they real?' Lydia asked.

'Yes, and no one likes them because they are grey and make all your clothes smell no matter how long you air them.'

'Could we ask your sprite friends, Bel?' said Bertie. 'They might know what to do.'

'They'll only laugh at my old noggin for being caught out on St Nick's night! And anyway, no sprite is allowed to help another grant a wish, it's a rule. The only thing that can help me is granting this stuck wish! What have we learnt so far about Lydia's mother? Bertie, now you know all about the wish-tastrophe I'm in, you can help us! Lydia, didn't you say Lady Partridge was talking about your ma at the ball?'

'Yes,' said Lydia doubtfully. 'At least I *think* she was – they were talking about a Catherine, but it might not have been my mother—'

'It must be!' Bel exclaimed. 'So Lady P did know

her, or met her at least!'

'But she told me in the carriage she didn't. I don't know, Bel, I can't ask any more questions just now, she's already so cross with me. But perhaps if we found the ruby necklace and proved Bertie's innocence, Lady Partridge might be in a better mood and then we could ask more questions about my mum?' Lydia took a deep breath and told them her new theory. 'I was thinking. Ronalds was horrible to Bertie in the kitchen, just gleeful that he had been branded a thief. I bet he knows something about the ruby and was glad someone else was being blamed!'

Bel shook her head and her skirt began to smoke again. 'Snail trails and slug nibbles – another mystery! And it doesn't have anything to do with your mother. If my wand was working properly I'd turn your feet into ducks and watch you waddle about, but since I can't do that … fine, let's go and look for clues. Not that it will help us solve our wish.' She rolled her eyes.

'We'd better find something soon or I shall use my last remaining bit of magic to singe your eyebrows off so you can never look surprised!"

'Miss Lydia,' said Bertie gently. 'I still don't understand. How will finding out more about your mum and how she knew Lady P help her to "come back"? How will it grant the wish?'

Lydia let out a big sigh. 'I don't know, Bertie. But we have to keep trying. Bel needs us.'

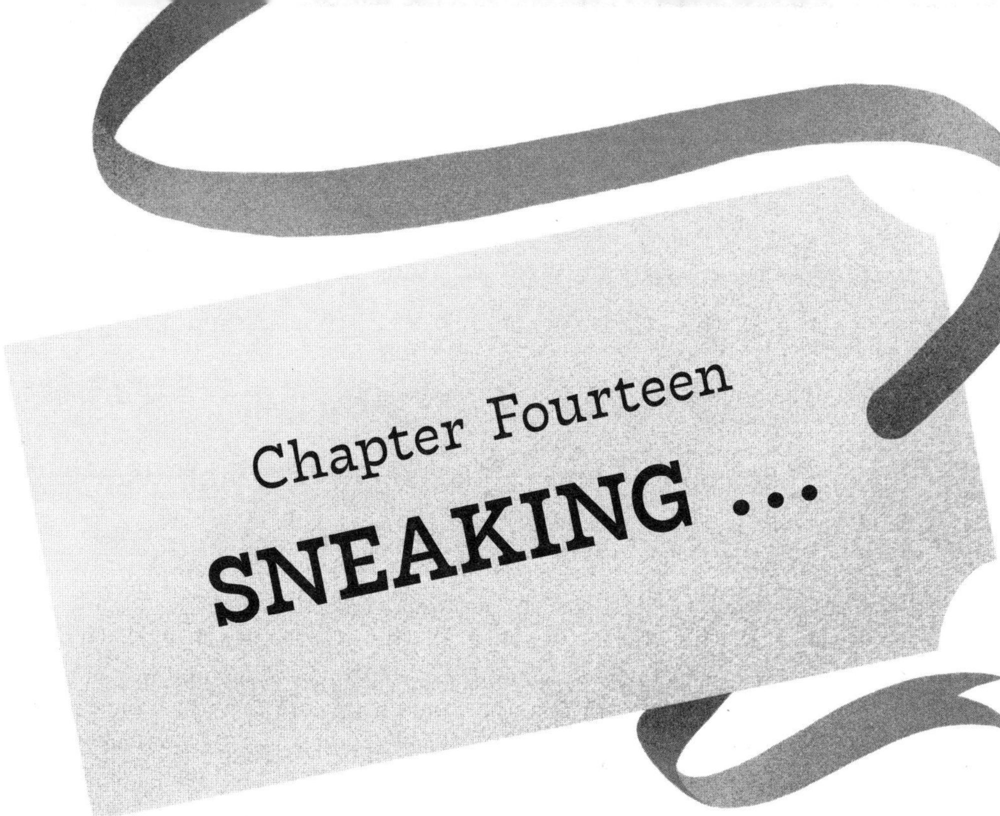

Chapter Fourteen
SNEAKING ...

The next morning Lady Partridge and Ronalds left for Bath, in search of yet more wedding clothes, or hats, or feathers, and various other pieces she said were essential for her wedding outfit.

Lydia and Bel had agreed to meet Bertie at the bottom of the servants' quarters stairs, as soon as they heard the carriage trotting away. 'Psst!' Lydia whispered. 'Bertie?'

'Don't say my name!' he whispered back, stepping out of a doorway and double-checking the coast was clear before running over to her. 'What if someone hears us?'

'Well, what *should* I call you?' asked Lydia.

Bel hauled herself out of Lydia's pocket, climbed up on to her shoulder and held on to her ear to steady herself. 'Lydia should be Conker and Bertie should be Acorn. Because you're both silly nut-heads who are about to land somewhere you shouldn't.'

Bertie and Lydia looked at each other. Lydia knew Bel was right; the past week had finally been trouble-free, and she was getting nearer to passing her trial with every day that passed. But Ronalds had been awful to her since the day she arrived. He *wanted* her to fail her test and be sent away, and now it seemed he wanted to get rid of Bertie too. He was what her mum would have called a 'bad egg'. Surely he was up to no good?

They **crept** down the stairs to the servants' quarters. Lydia had only been in the kitchen before,

which was so full of Harriet it always felt **welcoming**. The rest of the quarters were very different. Lydia was surprised at how small the rooms were: a quarter of the size of her bedroom upstairs. She saw Martha's room, which was as tidy as she was, but Lydia felt sad to see so few possessions and not even a window. There were two beds and Lydia realised Martha must share with another serving girl. There were so many staff who kept Peppomberley going, yet she only knew a few of them by sight. Even when she had tried to smile at someone passing in the corridor, they would **nod politely** and rush past, probably scared to make conversation in case Ronalds caught them and unleashed one of his **infamous** tellings-off.

In Hopperton Lydia had taken the time to always smile or speak to everyone in the village, no matter who they were, but she'd learnt at Peppomberley there was a difference. It didn't seem right or fair, but questioning it was surely another way to anger Lady Partridge. A *proper lady* shouldn't tell their superiors when they are wrong, Martha had told her.

Bertie of course knew this bit of the house well and led Lydia to the end of the corridor – Ronalds' room. The door was ajar, and they slipped in. The room was larger than Martha's, but housed only a simple bed, a desk and a chair that looked old and worn but comfy. Everything was spotlessly clean, not a speck of dust. Lydia felt a pang of guilt but she pushed it away, thinking of Ronalds' cruel smile at Bertie last night in the kitchen. If he was hiding something that might help Bertie, they had to find it, or at least try. She carefully looked in the desk, but each drawer just had papers, letters and envelopes in – no ruby necklaces.

Lydia glanced at one of the envelopes stuffed into a drawer, and noticed it had been returned to Ronalds, which was odd. The letter was poking out and she could just read the sign-off. '. . . *with love evermore, your darling, Ronalds x*'. The idea of Ronalds being in love with someone was very strange to imagine. She resisted the temptation to read more – it was clearly private.

Bel jumped down off Lydia's shoulder and looked around the room with disdain. 'Nothing here but clean boots and stale air! Not even a welcome bowl of acorns for visiting squirrels. The man clearly doesn't have basic manners. Let's go!'

'Hang on, Conker.' Bertie slid himself under the bed so only his feet were sticking out. Lydia checked down the corridor once more for anyone coming.

Bel hopped over to a candle and began picking off chunks of wax and throwing them over her shoulder.

'Bel! Don't do that,' hissed Lydia. 'He'll know someone has been here!'

'Then you shouldn't have been nosy foxes and come poking around!' she said.

Just then, there was a **bang** from outside the room. Lydia **jumped** out of her skin as Bertie sat up too quickly, bashing his head on the bed frame.

'What was that?' he asked.

'I don't know!' hissed Lydia. She peeked through the gap in the door and saw, further down the corridor, the back of a man, **darting** between the rooms, clearly as nervous about being there as they were. She saw a flash of black curly hair, but didn't have any time to think who was down there with them.

'Someone's coming!' she whispered. 'There's nowhere to hide in here, and we can't go back the way we came.' She could feel her heart pounding. If Lady Partridge found out she'd been **snooping**, she'd be at the workhouse before nightfall, and Bel would never get home, and Bertie would surely go to prison, and—

'Conker!' Bertie grabbed her shoulders and gave them a gentle shake. 'There's a small door opposite this one. I'm not sure where it leads, but maybe we can hide in the stairwell until whoever is rummaging around has gone?'

Bertie and Lydia looked at each other and both took a deep breath. They heard an even nearer door open and shut. It was now or never. Lydia pulled the door open and **dashed** across the corridor, not daring to look around, and flung open the other door. Bertie **barrelled** into her and they landed in a heap at the foot of a narrow spiral staircase. They quickly recovered themselves and ran upwards. The narrow stairs curved up towards a small window in the side of the wall. Lydia glanced out and to her horror saw Lady Partridge's carriage returning.

'Acorn! They're back already!' Lydia gasped. Lady Partridge marched out of the carriage, clearly shouting at Ronalds. 'They must have forgotten something!'

They surged faster up the stairs, neither she nor Bertie having any idea where they were heading. The passage led to another tiny door, which, after a shove from Bertie, opened into a **huge** room.

Dust sheets covered wooden packing boxes and the windows were boarded up, so only slits of sunlight shone through. A huge chandelier hung in the middle of the room, and piled up against the sofas were several large paintings, covered by more sheets. A mouse darted between two big boxes stuffed with straw and disappeared into the wainscotting.

'Where are we?' said Bertie.

'It must have been the ballroom at some point,' Lydia said. 'It's beautiful.'

The windows looked out on to the formal gardens, so she could roughly sense where they were in the house. They needed to leave before they were discovered somewhere else they weren't meant to be.

A cloud of dust **billowed** into the air, causing Lydia to cough. Bel had pulled a dust sheet off one of the paintings.

'Bel!' Lydia scolded. 'What on earth do you think you're doing?'

'Searching for clues the proper way! And looks like I've found a good one.' She pointed at the painting. It depicted two girls in ornate dresses, with flowers and curls hanging down their shoulders. One was in blue and was clearly a young Lady Partridge, instantly recognisable from her huge brown eyes. Her face looked so optimistic and serene, nothing like the scowl and steely eyes Lydia had become accustomed to being the recipient of. The other girl was wearing a yellow dress and blue shawl, with a slight smile on her face. Lydia couldn't stop looking at that smile.

Her attention was broken by Bel hopping up and down and pointing.

'Oh, my giddy aunts and uncles, she looks like you! But less messy,' declared Bel. 'Like you had a polish! I didn't know humans had magic that powerful!'

Lydia took a **deep** breath.

'Well, it's not me.' She paused and gazed again at the girl in the painting. **'It's my mum.'**

Chapter Fifteen
ESCAPE

The three of them **stared** at the painting. Lydia was happy to see her mum again, especially like this, in a way she never had before. But next to Lady Partridge, in such finery? Why was she even *in* the painting?

'This is it, Miss Lydia Marmalade! We have found her! I can go home!' Bel called out, doing a cartwheel.

'But Bel, it's just a painting. I don't think that will grant the wish, will it?'

'Painting schmainting burbainting! You wished your mum was here with you and here she is.'

Lydia couldn't disagree with her. But this wasn't her mum, this was Catherine, someone Lydia had never met.

Bel was shaking her bum and trying to fluff her skirt up. A few sparks *pfutted* off it, but it didn't look ablaze as it had when they first met.

'I'm not sure it's worked, Bel,' said Lydia.

'Nonsense and horse chestnuts! I'm just a bit smoked out. Give it a few hours and I'll be ready to fly home! Gosh, the place will need a good clean, and I'll have to order in some more magic ingredients too, I've not a jot of moonlight dust—'

'Sshh,' said Bertie. 'I can hear someone! They're coming the same way we did!'

Lydia threw the sheet back over the painting, then they rushed over to the grand doors, only to find them locked.

'Bel!' hissed Lydia. 'Have you any magic left?'

Bel looked doubtfully at the lock. 'Not much, Lyds, as you very well know. But I might have enough to …' She gave her wand a big knock on the floor and some pale sparks **spluttered** out. 'I'll have to tell it what to do,' Bel harrumphed. She aimed the wand at the lock, then began to hop up and down. There was a small *pop*, and then the lock turned into a tiny frog! It hopped out of the door and into Bertie's hands, leaving just a hole.

'*That* was astonishing, Bel!' whispered Lydia, as they opened the doors and found themselves on a huge landing. Lydia reached into her pocket – she had brought her father's compass, just in case. She had memorised which way it pointed when she was in different bits of the house. She let the golden needle settle and worked out where they were. **'This way!'** She pointed.

She led Bertie across the landing and down another

flight of stairs, checking the needle as they changed directions. They rounded a corner and Lydia could see they were a stone's throw from the main entrance.

'I know where I am now, Conker.' Bertie gave her a wink. 'I'd better get back to the stables quick smart.'

He **disappeared** down the stairs and into the servants' entrance, still holding the tiny frog in his hands.

Lydia let out a huge sigh. They had made it! They hadn't found the necklace, but they had found something else important – something which might be a clue to the link between her mother and Lady Partridge. But how could she ask Lady Partridge about the painting without giving away that she'd been in the ballroom?

Lydia was about to take herself and Bel back to her room for a long think, when she heard a **sob** coming from the hallway. She **peeked** through the banisters. She could see a figure at the front door. It was Marianne! She was trying to gather her bonnet and shawl and open the door at the same time, when suddenly Edmund called out, 'Marianne! Wait!' He was out of breath and trying to catch up to her. 'Don't go!'

She turned and smiled at him, but still tears poured down her cheeks. Lydia held her breath and Bel peered over her pocket. Marianne went to say something but stopped herself, and instead hurried through the open door to her waiting carriage. Edmund hung his head and Lydia saw him wipe his face.

'For rich people, they don't half cry a lot,' said Bel, shaking her head. Lydia couldn't help but silently agree.

Finally back in her room, Lydia placed Bel, who was almost asleep by now, into her window nest. The energy of the morning's shenanigans had wiped her out again, and she slept like a baby.

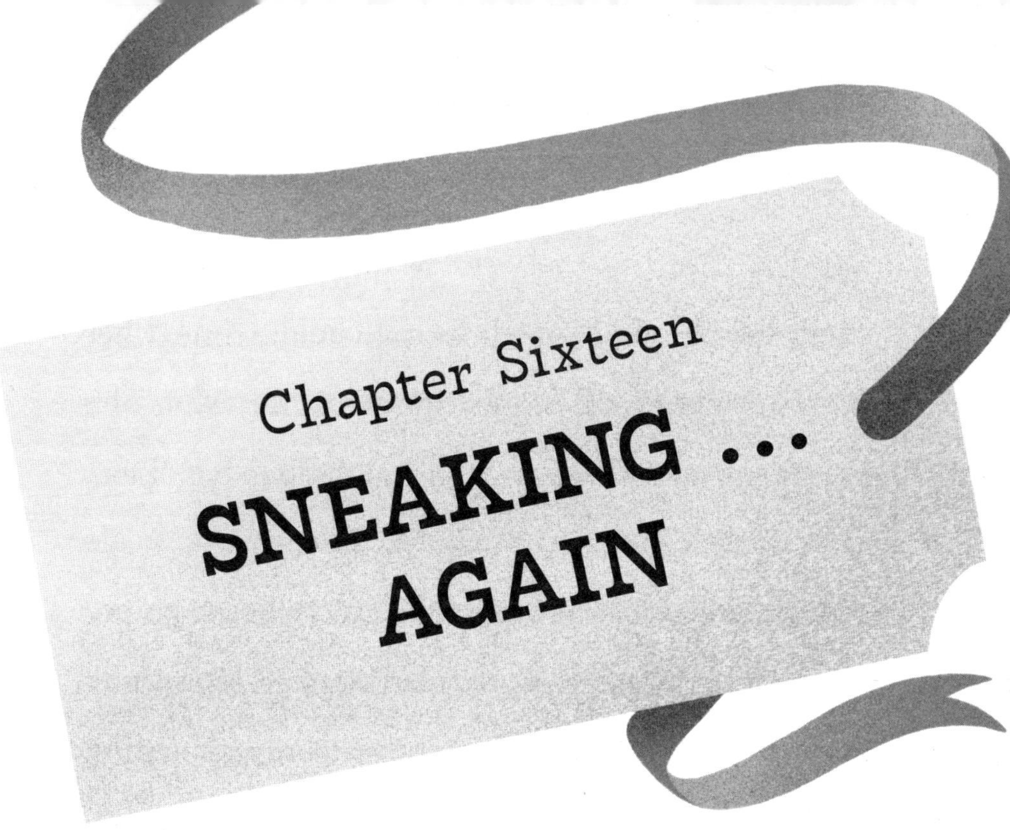

Chapter Sixteen
SNEAKING ... AGAIN

That night Lydia woke with a start. The moon was high, and the night sky was still black. Bel was fast asleep, lightly snoring to herself. Lydia took big deep breaths and tried to go back to sleep, but her brain was too busy. Why was there a painting of her mother and Lady Partridge? Had Lady Partridge been her mother's friend? The questions gathered and circled her mind and wound their way around her eyes, propping them open, till Lydia had no choice but to get out of bed.

It was freezing and she wrapped herself in as many shawls and blankets as she could, opened her bedroom door and padded down the corridor. She took a candle with her, and her father's compass. Even though she knew the house quite well now, she still felt scared walking around it in the quiet, empty night. Peppomberley in the dark looked even more imposing, the large columns in the front hall casting huge shadows as she passed them.

Lydia took out the compass, found her way back to the ballroom and pushed open the heavy wooden doors, still open and now in need of a new lock. Heading straight to the painting, she carefully took the sheet down and set the candle in front of it. 'Hello, Mum,' she said quietly to the brushstrokes and, although she longed for something to change, the figures in the painting stayed exactly where they had been. She stared at her mother, the dress, the flowers, the hair. She got up close to the face and gently touched its cheek. Lydia noticed Lady Partridge's hand resting on her mother's shoulder, how happy they looked together. Why had Lady Partridge said that she hadn't known her? Why did she lie?

The winter wind whistled against the thin glass windows and Lydia wished she had Bel or Bertie with her. She looked harder at her mum and smiled back. She understood why Bel had thought this would count. The portrait of her mother wasn't what she had wished for – it wasn't a hug, a hand, the sound of her laughing, watching her cooking Lydia's favourite pudding – all those things had gone, of course. But it *was* like seeing her again, in a way.

Lydia sighed. Suddenly she felt very tired. She started to gather her cold bones into the shawls to leave – but just as she stood up, she heard the sound of someone trying the locked the door, followed by a confused-sounding, 'What the—?'

It was Edmund!

Lydia blew the candle out and dived behind a sofa. She hadn't had time to throw the sheet over the painting, but she held her breath and hoped she wouldn't be found. Why was Edmund still wandering all over the house? What was he looking for?

The door opened. She could hear footsteps walking slowly but purposefully across the room. She peered from behind the sofa and could make out Edmund pushing a particularly large packing box to one side.

Lydia saw there was a cabinet behind it. Edmund reached into his pocket and then she saw a flash of red – the ruby necklace!

Lydia gave a squeal of shock and placed her hand over her mouth, making herself as small as she could.

'Who's there?' he whispered into the dark.

Edmund waited, stock still, until he shook his shoulders, and muttered, 'Mice,' to himself. He placed the necklace in a drawer and pushed the huge case back in front of it.

Edmund was the thief! He had been looking for somewhere to hide the necklace all this time. But why? *He* didn't need it. He was rich enough, wasn't he? And Marianne was so sad about it – why wouldn't he just give it back to her?

Edmund! She needed to get back and tell Bel and Bertie as soon as possible!

Chapter Seventeen
CHRISTMAS EVE

As the weak sun crept through the window, Lydia was not ready to face the morning. Bel was already up and looking fresher than usual.

'It's the Christmas spirit! I can smell it! 'Tis Christmas Eve! If I were home now, I would be roasting chestnuts and pickling parsnips and wrapping my hair with holly leaves!' Bel said, marching up and down the windowsill, sweeping it with a broom she had made with twigs and feathers

Lydia had brought her.

Christmas Eve. Lydia realised she was nearly through her trial period, and Lady Partridge hadn't thrown her out for failing to be a 'proper lady' – yet. She was so close, but right now she couldn't stop thinking about Edmund. Why had he stolen the necklace?

She sat up and told Bel everything. After she had finished, Bel did a handstand against her bed nest. 'What are you doing?' Lydia asked.

'If you have evidence that Edmund is the thief, that could save Bertie Boo. But what you just told me has scrambled my brain so much I'm turning my noggin upside down to put it all back in the right place!'

Lydia **giggled**, but she thought Bel had a point. If everyone knew the truth, then Bertie would be safe. But could Marianne **forgive** Edmund, or would she call off the wedding? And what would Lady Partridge say? It was too much for Lydia to think about. She **sank** back into her bed and pulled the covers over her face.

***

As Lydia and Bel entered the kitchen, Harriet was already starting preparations for the Christmas Day feast. Pots were boiling and the most delicious smells were coming from the oven. Colin **bounded** over to them, and Lydia noticed he was rounder than before. 'Harriet, he looks as if he's been enjoying your cakes a little too much!'

Colin **snorted** and **licked** his lips, pushing his head under her hand, so she was tickling his ears without even realising it.

Lydia saw Bertie in the garden and rushed outside to tell him her news, Colin bounding after her. Bel climbed out of Lydia's pocket and placed herself on Lydia's shoulder as Lydia explained what had happened.

'It makes no sense, Lyddy!' said Bertie angrily. 'Why, if you hadn't seen him with your own eyes, I would never have believed it!'

'I know! Why on earth would Edmund want Marianne's necklace?' Lydia agreed.

'You should go up to him and give the rascally raspberry a right bonk on the nose!' Bel proclaimed.

'No!' both Lydia and Bertie said at the same time and then they couldn't help it, they all started giggling.

'You could stuff his shoes with snails or get a badger to fart in his bed – they do the most awful smells, worse even than weasels!' snorted Bel.

'I wish we could do those things,' said Lydia, 'but Edmund is a gentleman.' She looked at each of them. 'Accused by an orphan, a stable boy and a – sprite? No one would believe us.'

Bel **stomped** her foot. 'Nothing makes any sense, Lyddy Loo!' She counted on her tiny fingers. 'A old collar belonging to Lady P for a dog called Colin, who is not *our* Colin, but an old long ago Colin. Lady P seems to know your mum but her tongue's been magicked off every time you ask her about it. Edmund stole the rubies but we can't tell anyone because of your silly human rules. And I'll never get my magic back unless I can make it feel like your mum is here and all the while my magic is turning to ashes as we sit here like eggs with no nest!'

'Bel, could we ask your sprite friends to help us?' suggested Lydia. 'Or Stanley the squirrel? We can find them and explain—' She hopped up to the first branches of a nearby tree and looked out towards the woods.

Bertie took out the tiny frog that Bel had magicked in the ballroom. 'What about Ted?' Lydia and Bel stared at him and he blushed. 'I called him that. Bet he could go back and find some of your pals and tell them—'

'No no no!' Bel cried. 'Don't you either of you be telling any woods folks what's happened to me! This is why all the winter sprites stopped helping you big peoples, you're all so silly and mixed-up! Edmund's done wrong and we have done right! I'm going to tell them all it was that silly goose who took those red gems.' Bel flapped her wings and **zoomed** off into the air.

'Bel!' Lydia shouted after her.

'She can't go far without you, can she?' asked Bertie, carefully putting Ted back in his pocket.

'No, I think the pull will stop her going too far. She's been so weak, I'm surprised she's managed to fly!'

'Where's she off to?' asked Bertie. 'She can't just appear in front of Lady Partridge and tell her what's going on!'

But Lydia wasn't paying attention. She had noticed some letters carved on the tree at exactly her height. 'Bertie, look at this! It says … *G* + *C*, I think. Who do you think can have carved that? No one else around here climbs trees.'

Before Bertie could come and see, Harriet stuck her head out of the back door and called, 'Miss Lyddy, Lady Partridge is calling for you, my duck!'

Lydia gave Bertie a look and ran back to the house. Surely Bel couldn't have told Lady Partridge already!

Chapter Eighteen
CARRIAGE CONVERSATIONS

Lydia **ran** up the front stairs to meet Lady Partridge and by the time she got to the hallway she was red-faced and panting. Lady Partridge gave her a **disdainful** look.

'A lady never runs, Miss Marmalade. May I suggest you are simply *on time*?' Lady Partridge continued to put on her large bonnet and gloves.

'But – I – didn't – know – I – was – late!' Lydia countered.

'We are going to the Firths for a Christmas Eve card party,' said Lady Partridge.

Lydia could see from Lady Partridge's attire this was a sudden decision. She was in her second-best dress, with only three feathers in her hair.

'Now, wear these,' Lady Partridge commanded, handing Lydia a new shawl and bonnet. Lydia was **reluctant** to take her mother's shawl off – wearing it felt like protection somehow – but perhaps this meant she would pass the trial, since Lady Partridge had spent money on her. Or was it just to keep up appearances for the Firths? Either way, she knew she should be grateful for the generosity being shown. 'Thank you, Lady Partridge.' Lydia tried her curtsey again, but nearly **wobbled** over.

Lady Partridge **narrowed** her eyes and then shouted, **'Edmund!'**

Lydia froze. What on earth could she say to him, knowing he was the thief?

He walked towards them, head down. 'Mother, I have told you already, I will not come with you to a party, with everything that is happening—'

'And I have told *you*, Edmund, not to mope! We shall go to the Firths', everyone will see you are quite well and that Ma— that whatever happened with the engagement is not your fault, and we shall sail into the spring as planned.' She looked at him **firmly**.

'No, Mama. As head of the household, no, I will not.' Edmund walked away, with an expression on his face which Lydia couldn't read.

Lady Partridge looked like she might explode with rage, but she managed to contain it. She called after him, 'Fine! Then Miss Marmalade and I shall attend and I shall tell them you are being sick so constantly, you have turned quite green!' She **threw** the door open and stomped down the grand stairs to the awaiting carriage. 'Marmalade! Follow! Ride fast, thank you, driver, I do not wish to add lateness to the reasons we are being gossiped about!'

The coach driver gave her a nod and Lydia saw Bertie was also at the driving seat attending to the horses. He looked at Lydia, clearly wondering whether Lady Partridge knew the truth yet. She shook her head ever so slightly.

Lydia was worried about Bel and what would happen if she left without her. The familiar pull she felt when they were too far apart wasn't there, but where was Bel? She scanned around one last time to try and spot the sprite before stepping into the carriage.

Bertie gave a shout to the horses to trot on.

***

They were silent for some time. Lydia felt herself starting to drift off, still tired from the shenanigans the night before, when Lady Partridge suddenly blurted out, 'What could he have *done*?'

Lydia was confused.

Lady Partridge continued. 'What has Edmund done to make Marianne break the engagement?'

Lydia gasped. So that's why Edmund had looked so upset yesterday. Marianne had broken off the engagement! Had Marianne found out that he'd stolen the necklace? Was that why?

'Is not Edmund a handsome, kind and wealthy catch? It makes no sense to me, no sense at all! It can't all be because of this absurd necklace business! Dreadful Lady Braun is claiming that's the reason and she wants nothing to do with our family, but anyone with any sense can see Marianne was dancing with it one moment and then it was gone the next. She must simply have lost it!'

Lydia didn't know what to say. She wanted to shout out, *it was Edmund who took it!* But the words wouldn't come out of her mouth.

'I don't know why Lady Braun is determined to go on about that necklace anyway!' continued Lady Partridge. 'She has agreed not to call the constable in for Bertie, so that is something at least.'

Lydia gasped. 'Oh, so Bertie is safe, then! I always said he didn't do it.'

'So relentlessly *hopeful*, Lydia,' tutted Lady Partridge. 'But until the necklace is found we will not have any peace.' She turned away, saying quietly to herself, '*Happiness falls where it wants, no matter how fine your purse is.*' Her mother's favourite saying, Lydia thought with a jolt.

The carriage drove on out of the forest and past the fields, towards the Firths, who Lydia knew were their nearest neighbours, kind but not nearly grand enough for Lady Partridge to spend much time with.

Lydia had never wanted to come to Peppomberley, that was true, but thanks to Harriet, Bertie and even Bel, somehow she and Colin had managed to fit in, in a way she had never thought would be possible. Here Lydia was, alone with Lady Partridge – she should at least try to find out some answers about her mother – something that might help Bel. She took a deep breath.

'Lady Partridge?' Lydia asked quietly. 'I'm sorry to be bold, but I wanted to ask you something, if you don't mind. It's about my mother. Um, I know you said you'd never met before, but perhaps you're mistaken? Maybe you did know each other when you were younger and you've just forgotten?'

Lady Partridge turned to her abruptly. 'I did not

know your mother, Lydia. I never forget anything. She was a distant relative by marriage, and I felt pity for your plight, that is all. That subject is now closed.'

She didn't look at Lydia for the rest of the journey.

Chapter Nineteen
CARDS

They arrived at the Firths' house and Lydia was **immediately** struck by how much smaller it was than Peppomberley, and how grand Lady Partridge looked there. Her bonnet alone was twice the size of anyone else's and Lydia could tell she was enjoying this as she didn't take it off for some time.

Mrs Firth was an elegant and gracious host who welcomed them both in **wholeheartedly**. She complimented Lady Partridge on her outfit and even said she had heard much about Lydia (although whether it was good or bad was not clear).

Mrs Firth took Lady Partridge into the drawing room, where a card party was forming. Everyone was polite to Lydia, but there was not much for her to do.

She sat down at a window seat and watched the grey clouds darken as the party wore on, listening to a group sitting next to her. It was mostly village **gossip**, but every now and again Lydia recognised a name and would listen carefully so she could report back to Harriet, who loved to know what everyone was up to. George the butcher had been caught hiding chickens as pets; he liked them so much he would not sell them. Lady Arabella de Whitt had fainted after purchasing such a large hat her head could not bear the weight. Then Lydia's ears really pricked up, as they began to discuss Lady Braun.

'Oh, 'tis a shame!'

'Oh, 'tis! 'Tis indeed!'

'Such a fine lady as Lady Braun to be so distressed! She is of course begging Marianne to marry Edmund, but Marianne refuses and no one knows why!'

Lydia couldn't **believe** her ears. If Lady Braun still wanted the marriage, the problem couldn't be anything to do with the missing necklace!

'Apparently Marianne herself spends all day weeping but she will not say why she has broken it off!'

The women began to discuss little Poppy the Jack Russell terrier, who had been crowned the best-dressed dog in the county at the winter fair, despite suspicions she had help with her costume from her owner Mrs Mitcham, the tailor ...

Lydia was preparing to spend the rest of the evening bored stiff when she heard a commotion. Miss Susan Firth, Mrs Firth's eldest daughter, was **flapping** around and **screeching**.

'An enormous moth! Or something! It fell out of

your bonnet, Lady Partridge!' squealed Susan.

'A moth! What are you talking about, child! I had no such thing in my hat! How ridiculous!' Lady Partridge looked furious.

Bel! She must have been hiding in Lady Partridge's hat! Lydia looked **frantically** around the table and on the floor.

Lady Partridge stood up, shaking herself and her gloves out. Miss Firth looked most ashamed but tried to defend herself. 'I saw tiny yellow sparks – they fell down from your hat—' but as she carried on even she doubted herself. 'Maybe it was a sparkly spider … ?'

And then Lydia saw her. Under the table, one of the Firths' spaniels was sniffing something that did look like a moth, so brown and papery was its appearance. It was Bel. Lydia **scooped** her up and gently wrapped her in a linen napkin.

'What have you got, Miss Marmalade?' Miss Firth asked nervously.

'Oh, just some crumbs to take out to the – to the – um, to the sprites.' She could think of nothing else to say.

Lady Partridge rolled her eyes. 'Really Lydia, to believe in such silliness, you sound like your mo—' She stopped herself.

'Like who?' said Lydia, her hands shaking.

'Like no one!' Lady Partridge swished herself back down into her card game and Lydia ran outside.

She knew **exactly** what Lady Partridge was about to say – her mother! Here she was lecturing her on how to be a lady, telling her to be good and honest, and then lying right to her face. Lydia felt her face flush with anger. Bertie was outside checking on the horses and she raced towards him.

Before he could say anything, Lydia held up the napkin and said, **'Bel!'**

He gestured to follow him and led Lydia into the garden. It had just started to snow and she laid the napkin down on to the stone wall. Lydia uncovered Bel and let out a gasp. It was Bel, but her skirt was now completely grey; it was starting to fall apart, **disintegrate**, it was becoming ashes. Lydia froze. She knew what this meant, she had known for days. Bel was very unwell. What was worse than this? To lose Bel after all she'd been through, and knowing it would be her fault was **unbearable**.

Bertie picked Bel up as gently as he could, and he held the tiny sprite to his ear. 'She's still breathing, Miss Lyddy. But it's slow. Get some of them dry leaves from over there.' Lydia gathered as many as she could, and gently wrapped Bel in them.

'Smell of trees should help,' said Bertie.

'It's not enough, Bertie. We need to *do* something!'

Lydia looked all around. There was nothing else

that wasn't already covered in the light sprinkling of snow, it was all so cold and wet. She knew she didn't have long. She stared at the carriage.

'Bertie. I need to borrow the carriage.'

'Miss Lydia! You can't be serious! We can't take the carriage without Lady P and—'

'I have to! I'll take Bel back to her woods, I'll go and find Stanley. We have to *do* something!'

Bertie looked at the little leafy bundle and then gave a nod. 'You're not doing it without me, that's for sure.'

'But Bertie, you'll get into so much trouble—'

'So will you!'

Lydia smiled at him. It wasn't the proper thing to do – a ward and a stable boy and a sprite going off in a carriage that most certainly was not theirs to take. But Lydia knew: sometimes the *right* thing wasn't the *proper* thing to do, and that's why rules, sometimes, had to be broken.

'We need to go back to Peppomberley! That's where Bel's woods are – and Harriet will know what to do!' Lydia said.

Bertie took one look at the heavy gold carriage and the four horses tied to it.

'Miss Lydia, there's one way we can get there that's much faster.'

Lydia smiled. 'Then let's do it!'

'I need to tell her first, they don't like surprises.' Bertie unhooked the front horse. 'Mabel, we got a sprite that needs help here, we need to get her home.' Mabel let out a big snort of air and banged her hooves to the ground. 'Merlin, you stay here and make sure Lady P gets back in one piece!'

Bertie grabbed a blanket from the footman's perch and threw it on to Mabel's back. Lydia wrapped Bel up as best she could in her shawl and Bertie helped them both get on, grabbed Mabel's reins and gave a shout. They were off!

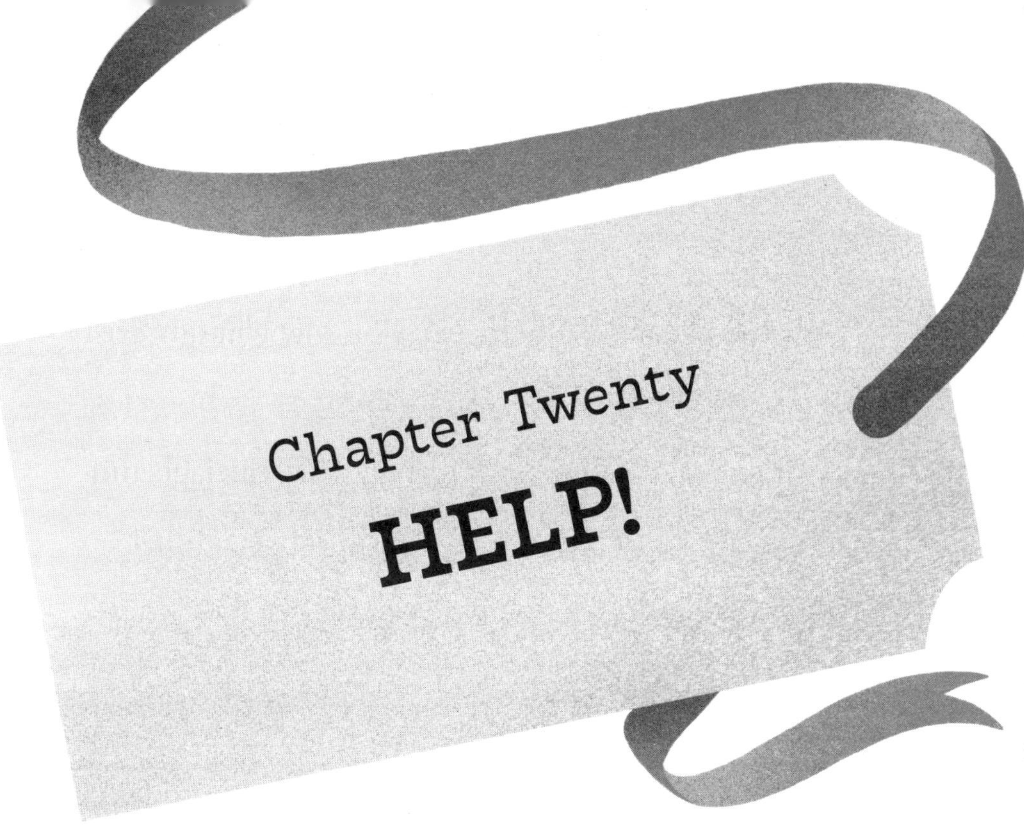

Chapter Twenty
HELP!

Bertie rode through the **dimming** light as fast as he could; Mabel knew the way, without his guidance. Lydia talked and talked to Bel as they rode, describing the winter trees, the stars and how much she was going to do in the spring, anything she could think of to keep her there. She tried not to think of Lady Partridge and the scene she had left behind her, though she did have time to tell Bertie the very good news about Lady Braun dropping her threat of calling the constable on him.

She knew that fleeing the party on Mabel might cost her everything, that she could be sent away, homeless at Christmas – but what was the alternative? Having a home but knowing in your heart that you didn't do everything you could to help your friend? That wasn't a life worth anything.

Mabel cantered up the drive to Peppomberley and Bertie steered them to the back of the house, right up to the kitchen door. Harriet ran out to them.

'Lyddy! Bertie! What are you doing? Where's Lady Partridge?'

'We don't have time, Auntie H!' Bertie **shouted** and they ran into the kitchen.

Colin began to **bark** and leap up as Harriet chased in after them. 'Now you tell me right now, Herbert, what you two are up to!'

'Oh, Harriet!' Lydia did the only thing she knew to be right, she told Harriet the truth. About Bel appearing the night she made the wish, about trying to find out how Lady Partridge knew her mother, and how none of their plans had worked and so Bel had got weaker and weaker, but she hadn't known how to help her. Tears poured down Lydia's face as she gingerly unwrapped Bel to show Harriet. Her skirt was dark grey now and little pieces of it were turning to **ash** and **crumbling** away. Bel looked very peaceful, as if she was asleep, and Lydia could hear her muttering, 'The summer woods, I've got to find them …'

Harriet took one look at the poor sprite and took Lydia firmly by both arms. 'Lyddy, go to the pantry and fetch the big jar full of conkers, bring them to me and chuck them in the pot. Bertie, I need holly berries, a snowdrop – although it's early …' She looked worried. 'A snowdrop if you can, if not, then ivy leaves and evergreens, lots of them.'

She put the leaves in a pudding bowl before gently laying Bel in them. 'You did right to put her in the leaves. She's been too long from nature, Lyddy, it's not good for sprites to live with us.'

'But can we help her, Harriet? Can we save her?' The words stuck in her throat.

'We'll do our best, Lyddy. Now go.'

Lydia gathered the conkers and watched as Harriet began to boil them up, slicing them out of the skins as the water got hotter. Lydia followed Harriet's instructions as she pounded rosehips into a paste and added hot conker water to make tea. She held a tiny wooden spoon up to Bel's lips and managed to get some into her.

Bel let out a tiny sigh as the warm pink liquid went down, like medicine. Lydia **squeezed** her eyes to stop the tears.

Bertie returned with a bushel of leaves and the tiniest snowdrop. 'It was only just out the ground, Auntie H, I wasn't sure I should take it …'

'Not normally, Bertie, but the wood will forgive you because it knows it's for one of its own,' Harriet said.

Lydia added the snowdrop petals to the tea and gave some more to Bel. Harriet toasted two crumpets, covered them in butter and jam, and gave them to Bertie and Lydia.

'No use everyone feeling hungry,' she said, and she let Colin **nibble** a little chunk from her hand.

Finally, Lydia had got most of the tea into Bel. She lifted her carefully and placed the ivy and evergreens underneath her so she now rested on a lush green nest of leaves. The whole kitchen smelt like the deepest part of the woods.

Lydia fetched moss from outside and placed it over Bel like a soft green blanket. Despite the freezing cold night, Harriet opened the window and placed the pudding bowl full of forest and Bel on the sill. 'She needs fresh air now. The fire might not come back full, Lyddy, but hopefully we can stop the flame going out completely.'

Lydia held Bel's tiny hand. It was still cool, but she could feel warmth coming back to it.

'We can do our best, but we won't get her magic back this way.' Harriet sat down and she poured herself some tea. 'That's strong wish magic. What exactly did you wish for that night, Lyddy?'

Lydia couldn't look at Harriet. 'I wished my mum was here with me.' Big fat tears dropped on to Bel and she tried to wipe them away.

'Don't worry, my love, tears of love and friendship won't harm her.'

'I am so sorry, Harriet! I didn't know anyone would hear me, it's just what I wanted most of all at that moment—'

'I'm sorry I told you to wish, Lyddy,' said Harriet. 'I should have been more careful. I knew you was missing your ma and I was trying to cheer you, but I should have let you miss her. You're allowed to miss someone when they're gone.'

Lydia looked at her and felt a well of gratitude that the world had given her Harriet, when she needed her most.

Bel stirred.

'Oh, that's a good sign, Lyddy! Take it easy now, Miss Bel, you've been too long from your magic, you're weaker than you'd like.'

Bel opened her eyes and looked at Harriet and then at Lydia and gave a little smile.

'Oh Bel!' whispered Lydia. 'I'm so sorry!'

Colin gave a quiet woof and settled down next to Harriet.

'I'll keep her near the winter air for as long as I can, but we need more than I can do,' said Harriet.

'What do you mean?' asked Lydia.

'Her friends. I'll leave some ivy wrapped in a circle on my doorstep and a candle at the window, oh and yes, some hawthorn on the gate too. That will bring them to us.'

'The other sprites?' Lydia asked.

'Some sprites, some pixies, some gnomes and this

near Christmas some elves too probably, getting ready to go north. Bel should have asked them for help a while ago – just as you should have asked me, but I understand why you were worried. Maybe Bel thought she got herself into a mess and she should get herself out. But that's not the way friends work.'

She gave Lydia a firm look and then pulled her in for a huge hug.

'Off to bed with you. And Bertie, go put Mabel in the stables, I'll send Fred with another horse to go to the Firths and pick up Lady Partridge. Ronalds will have some words with you in the morning too, no doubt.'

Bertie nodded and headed out the back door. Lydia gave one last look at Bel, and thought her cheeks were a bit rosier than they had been. She gave Colin a kiss and headed upstairs.

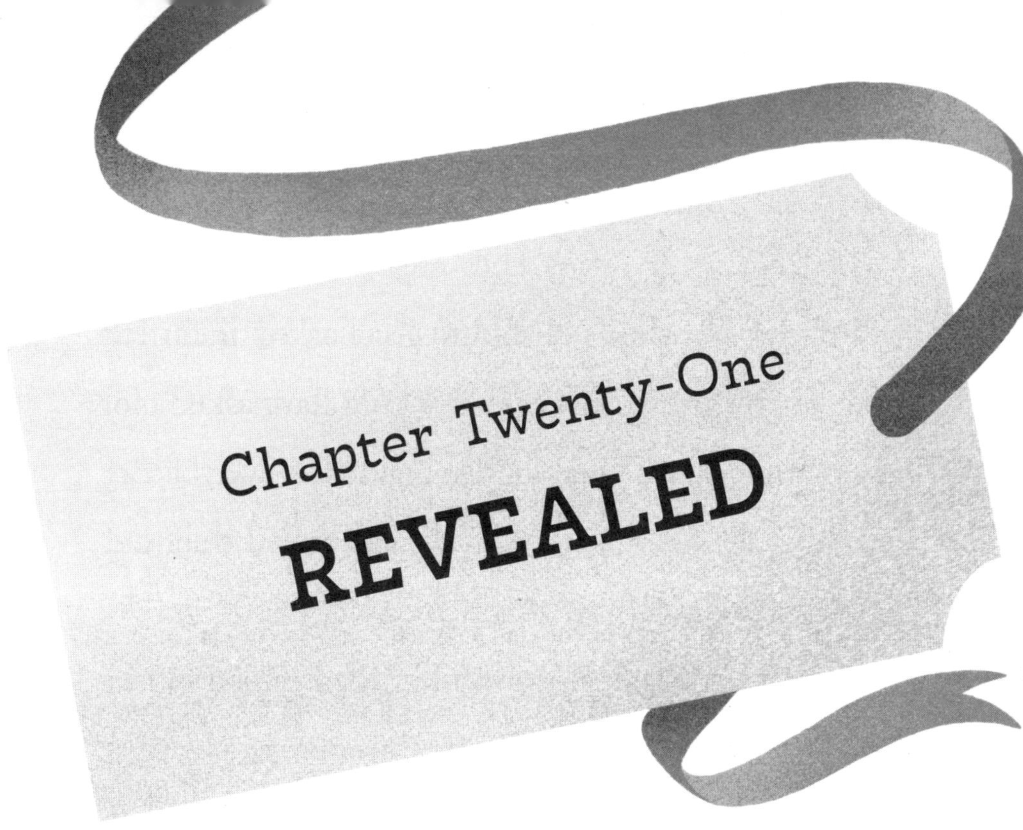

Chapter Twenty-One
REVEALED

Lydia sat in her room and looked out at the woods, hoping to see Bel's friends come to her aid. She had risked everything to help Bel, and yet – even with her friends' assistance – if she couldn't make the wish come true, she didn't know how long Bel's magic would last.

I wish my mum was here with me. That had been her wish. She needed to find a connection to her mum at Peppomberley, and see if that would make the wish feel true. But they'd been searching so hard, and all they'd found was an old dog collar, some initials carved on a tree (Lydia kept thinking about that C for Catherine) and a portrait. There was also the missing necklace and the fact that Edmund was a thief but Lydia wasn't sure how that helped Bel.

Still, Lydia couldn't stop thinking about the necklace – how telling the truth about Edmund would clear Bertie's name once and for all. She was in so much trouble now, having left Lady Partridge stranded, that things surely couldn't get any worse. She had to tell her. So what if Lady Partridge didn't believe her? Bertie was her friend and had risked so much to help her, and Bel. She had to at least *try*. But Lydia knew she needed evidence first. She picked up her candle and once more headed to the ballroom.

The cavernous room was as eerie as before, as the clock ticked towards midnight. She wanted to look at her mother again, but first crept over to the cabinet, determined to make things right. She opened the drawer – there was the necklace, the huge red gems sparkling in the candlelight. Lydia held it up to her neck and looked in a mirror on the wall. Yes, it was pretty, but all this trouble for a few shiny stones? She knew more than anyone that things didn't bring you happiness, only people – and, now, memories.

A creak in the hallway. Lydia could hear Lady Partridge's voice. She was back! 'Ronalds, I am quite well, and I will deal with Lydia in the morning.' She must surely be on her way to bed, at such a late hour. 'But I'm telling you, Ronalds, I've seen *several* frogs come out of this keyhole the last few days—' and the door swung open! There stood Lady Partridge and behind her, Ronalds. Both of them stared open-mouthed at Lydia, with the ruby necklace in her hands.

Lydia tried to speak, but Ronalds got there first.

'I knew it, ma'am! A bad and improper chit

from the moment she arrived!' Ronalds looked so **triumphant**, he was practically doing a jig. 'And here she is holding the stolen gems, as bold as brass!'

'Oh, Lady Partridge, I can explain!' Lydia gasped.

'Explain! Explain why you stole a horse, and left poor, defenceless Lady Partridge by herself *at the Firths of all places*!' Ronalds continued his gleeful rant.

'Yes, thank you, Ronalds,' Lady Partridge snapped. 'Do you have an explanation, child? I had none for my hosts as to why you and my horse had quite disappeared!'

Lydia **squirmed**. 'I'm sorry—' She knew they had done the right thing, but it was so hard to say it to Lady Partridge.

'And now this. Clearly it was *you*, Miss Marmalade, who took the necklace and were willing to let Bertie take the blame. I knew you were no born lady, but this behaviour is utterly unthinkable. It is not often I am wrong about anything, but it appears I misjudged you greatly.' Lady Partridge had an expression Lydia had not seen before, a look of **betrayal** and shock. Lydia felt quite sick.

'No – it's not what it looks like—'

'I have done everything I can to help you, but you do not want to be helped! You are a liar, and I can't abide liars. Pack your things. You shall be gone from Peppomberley tomorrow! Ronalds, lock the necklace in my desk.'

Ronalds **marched** towards Lydia and snatched the necklace out of her hands. He gave her a sneering look. 'Didn't make it to Christmas, Miss Marmalade,' he hissed. 'I believe I owe myself five shillings.' He slunk off, humming a carol to himself.

Lydia looked around, and her eyes settled on the painting, hidden by its dust sheet. There was her mother, here at Peppomberley, and Lydia knew she had nothing left to lose. *Be honest, Lydia.*

'Before I say goodbye, Lady Partridge, you should

know it was Edmund who stole the necklace. I saw him hide it here and wanted to return it to you.'

Lady Partridge **stared** at her, incredulous.

'And also,' Lydia took a deep breath, 'I haven't lied to you. I have done things I knew I shouldn't, but I haven't lied. Although you have.' She strode over to the painting and threw off the dust cover. 'You *did* know my mother, Lady Partridge. You knew her, and I have nothing left of her at all, and I only wanted a piece, something, even just a memory if that was all you had. I didn't want any money, or necklaces or fancy dresses. I wanted my mum back.'

Lydia wiped her face and waited for Lady Partridge's fury to hit her, but instead she looked pale.

'I haven't seen that painting for some time.' Lady Partridge's voice cracked and she slumped on to the sofa as though she'd been deflated.

'It is you? With her?' Lydia asked.

'Yes. Yes it's me, with my first cousin, Catherine. Your mother.'

***

Lydia pressed her lips together and took a deep breath. Her mum was Lady Partridge's cousin! Finally, the truth. But why had they pretended not to know each other?

Lady Partridge **sighed** and looked up at Lydia. Her hands were trembling, as if she was scared of Lydia, not the other way round. 'Catherine, your mother, was my cousin, and we were close as children. She stayed here often, and she was my friend. My dearest friend. But when she was older, she fell in love with a man who was very poor and her parents, my aunt and uncle, warned her – if she married him she would be removed from the family and no one would speak to her again. They thought that would stop her, but she was, as I'm sure you remember, determined. And she did marry him, and I never saw her again.'

Lydia breathed out, trying to understand everything. **'But my father, he died—'**

'Yes, they weren't married more than twelve months before he died, and then you came along. I thought maybe Catherine would come back to us then, but she didn't. She was cross with us all, me especially for not helping her when she needed it. She was right, of course, she often was. She always did what she thought was the right thing, no matter the consequences.'

Lydia felt her heart **swell** – her mum, yes, she did, she always did.

'It wasn't until she was sick that I heard from her again. She asked me to take you in. I agreed only if you didn't know the truth, otherwise I feared you would be angry with me. But that happened anyway.'

Lydia **blushed**.

'And I was concerned you would get into trouble, just like she had, so I set the trial for you, to teach you how to do things properly. We couldn't repeat your mother's mistakes! I'm sorry if I've been harsh, but you cannot survive in this world without knowing your station and sticking to the rules. I did not want you to end up with nothing, like your mother.'

Lydia slowly walked over to the sofa and sat down next to Lady Partridge. 'I think I'm beginning to understand. Only you've got it all wrong. My mother didn't end up with nothing. She was happy, with her home, her friends, with me.' Lydia paused, trying to push back down the lump in her throat.

Lady Partridge met Lydia's eye. 'Do you know, you sound like your mother? I missed her so much, Lydia. Losing her was like losing a sister. Seeing you has been wonderful and painful every day. Your mother would have missed all this,' she waved her arms around at the ballroom, 'but I see now, that wasn't what her heart needed. Perhaps it isn't what any of us *need*. You have been quite the reminder of that, Lydia.'

Lydia **stared** at her. She saw Lady Partridge was not scared *of* her, but afraid *for* her, about how Lydia would fit into the only world Lady Partridge had ever known.

'I'm – sorry,' she began. 'For all the trouble and the carriage. I had to get back, I was worried about – a friend—'

'Yes, Harriet did explain.'

'She … did?'

'Your friend who lives in the forest, who is sick? Harriet said that's why you came back.'

'Oh yes, that's true actually.'

'I'm sorry that I have not treated you as, well, as much like family as I should. Perhaps my dear departed husband would have helped me see that.' She let out a long sigh. 'Your mother gave me something, to be passed to you once you had been here a week and got to know us all.'

Lydia's heart **pumped** in her chest. One last missing piece of the puzzle … which might perhaps grant her wish?

'I should have given it to you, but I was anxious about what it might say, that you would find out the truth and not want to stay here.' Lady Partridge headed for the cabinet and opened another small drawer.

She handed Lydia an envelope. Lydia felt **warmth** spread across her chest. She desperately wanted to read it, but also knew these **magical** new words from her mum would only ever be new this once. She steeled herself and then slid the precious papers out. And there it was, her mother's beautiful looping handwriting.

A Guide to Surviving Peppomberley

Lydia laughed. The first page was a map, with all the twisting corridors and small doors marked on to it, and a tiny compass mark in the corner, so she could find her way round the house. Her mother had known she would start exploring straight away. There was another map of the formal gardens, and a beautiful sketch of the woods at the back. Underneath, her mother had noted, 'my favourite view of Peppomberley' – Lydia had stood on that very spot and felt the wind rush past her, seen how old and small Peppomberley had looked from there, and her mother had too. Lydia could even see some sparks flying up from the trees – maybe her mother had known about the sprites in the woods! There were more sketches and thoughts, a recipe for a pudding she liked, wildlife Lydia should look out for. And then, a letter on the last page.

My dearest Lydia,

I know you shall want to cause mischief in such a grand house. Peppomberley has that effect on some of us! I'm sure you have settled in now and that Georgiana (Lady Partridge to you) has told you the truth about how we knew each other, and lost each other. Underneath everything, she is the kindest soul, but not always the most willing to be silly until she is tricked into it – then I assure you she is more fun and trouble than even you are prepared for.

Enjoy Peppomberley, my darling girl. Whenever you need me, I am here – in the stars, in the roots of the trees, in the air all around you. I am not gone, I am in your heart beating with you. Miss me, Lydia, but do not ever feel alone.

Your loving mother xxxx

Lydia's heart was **thumping**. She looked up and saw Lady Partridge was wiping her eyes. **'I am so sorry I kept the letter from you.'**

Lydia smiled. It didn't seem to matter any more. 'Really, Lady Partridge, I forgive you.' She clutched the letter to her chest. 'Hearing Mum's voice again is like having her here with me, and that is all I wanted.'

'Thank you, Lydia – and please, call me Cousin Georgiana.'

Georgiana! Lydia had a flash of inspiration. 'Did you … ever climb trees when you and my mum were here together? Maybe even carve your initials into a tree?'

'Such vandalism! Certainly not,' Lady Partridge scoffed, giving Lydia a look that had more sparkle than Lydia had seen before. She took Lydia's hand and gave it a **gentle** squeeze. Lydia didn't know if she could ever call Lady Partridge 'Cousin Georgiana' or hug her like she did Harriet, but it was a different sort of love. Someone who knew her past and could help her make sense of it.

They sat in silence for a little while, until they heard the clocks strike midnight.

Lydia looked up. **'Happy Christmas!'**

Lady Partridge smiled. 'Happy Christmas, Lydia Marmalade.'

Chapter Twenty-Two
SPARKS

Lydia couldn't go to bed without seeing how Bel was doing, so once she'd wished Lady Partridge goodnight, she **crept** downstairs and slipped into the kitchen. Colin was asleep and snoring next to the range. Harriet was nowhere to be seen, but on the windowsill, surrounded by a warm glow, was a green pudding bowl with two feet sticking out the top, waggling their toes.

'Bel!' Lydia ran over to her. 'Bel! You are recovered?'

Bel opened one sleepy eye and smiled. 'Ah well, if it isn't Miss Lyddy Lou come to see me and myself!'

'How do you feel?'

'Oof, I have a fair headache, Miss Lyds, as if I drank a whole thimbleful of acorn wine! And I still feel as if my toes had an ice bath, but your hard work has been warming my cockles.' She laughed, and Lydia could hear the ripple of bells that she had heard the first time they'd met. Colin stirred in his basket and wriggled his legs in a dream.

'Oh, Bel, I'm so sorry ...'

'Sorry! What for? You silly chicken! You saved me! My fire was about to go out and if you hadn't helped me I'd be as dusty as the ashes in the fire grate this morn!'

'But it was my fault—'

'Oh me oh my. No no, I should have told you to find my friends quicker, but I was too proud, thought everyone would laugh at me for being caught on St

Nick's night, so I didn't want anyone to know. As stubborn as a leek sometimes I am. Stubborn as a leek.'

Bel stood up and her skirt was back to flames, **crackling** a dark, dark orange. Sparks were gently flying off her and her hair was the colour of holly berries again.

'Bel! Your magic is back!'

'Oh, my sparks and stars! Look at my dress, Lyddy Lou!' Bel jumped out of the bowl and did a very good forward roll. 'But that must mean your wish has been granted! Your ma! Is she here? Did you see her?'

'Not quite, Bel – but I know why she sent me, and I know that in some ways she'll always be here, at Peppomberley. That I might be able to make this my home.'

'My wand! I need to find the ol' thing!'

'I have it! I brought it with me in case you needed it.'

Lydia handed the wooden star stick back to Bel, and as soon as Bel held it out, thousands of tiny yellow **sparks** came off it like a firework. Bel let out a **hoot** of joy.

'Take that and party!' she shouted.

She aimed her wand at the dried herbs hanging down from the ceiling and suddenly the whole room smelt of rosemary, sage and thyme. There was a great sparkle of green and a *pop* and a tiny woven crown of leaves appeared and landed on Bel's head. Lydia **burst** out laughing.

'Bel! It works!'

Bel took a comically low bow and pointed her wand again. 'Don't think I'd forget you, Lyds—' She pointed the wand at the leaves in her bowl and they rose into the air, dancing around, forming a ring of winter leaves, sparkling green as Bel placed it on Lydia's finger, looking as serious as Lydia had ever seen her. 'A true friend ring, Lyds, forged from times of trouble and made solid to remind us of what we have been through and what we can survive.'

Lydia gave Bel's finger a little squeeze. 'Oh, Bel—'

'Now now, Lyds, don't make a fuss!' Bel turned her head and sneakily blew her nose on her wing.

'Bel, I'm so sorry for this wish-tastrophe. I should never have wished for something that was impossible.'

'That's what wishes are for, Lyddical! You can't wish for boring things you know will come true easily! You wished for your heart's greatest desire, and that's real magic.'

Bel's skirt **crackled** and **sparks** flew off it and singed the moss bed.

Lydia noticed a tiny parcel with an acorn poking out, wrapped up in some linen and attached to a small stick. Bel's possessions.

'Will you go home now, Bel?'

Bel looked a little **embarrassed**. 'I'm nots very good at goodbyes, Lyds, I normally leave a gathering without saying nothing to anyone – a sprite exit, they call it.' She twisted the wand around in her hands. 'I think I'm strong enough to go now.'

'Thank you, Bel. Thank you so much. I'm sorry I wished on you but I'm not sorry I met you.'

'Ah, you! You'll have me crying and putting out me fire again if you're not careful!' Bel gave Lydia a playful but quite hard kick on the knuckles. 'Now go and give that Edmund a double bonk on the nose, he deserves it!'

Lydia **laughed**. 'I'll look for you, Belamina Frosty Wonderlandus Sharp-Leaf, every St Nicholas Day. But I promise not to wish for anything too outrageous.'

'You can call for me any time. If you ever need me just leave out two pine cones on your windowsill and

I'll come.' Bel stuck out her hand and Lydia took it as best she could, hers being so much bigger, and shook on the deal. Then she watched as the tiny sprite flew out of the window, a **cascade** of sparks left suspended in the night air.

Chapter Twenty-Three
HOME

Lydia awoke. It was officially **Christmas Day**. Before she'd left Lady Partridge the previous night she had tried to explain again about seeing Edmund with the stolen necklace, but Lady Partridge (it still felt strange to think of her as Cousin Georgiana) was so tired she had simply waved her away and said they would speak of it tomorrow.

Just as Lydia was thinking of getting up, there was a loud **knock** on the door. It was Martha.

'Ronalds has told me you are to leave, miss!' She ran to Lydia and gave her a **huge** and most unexpected hug. 'Take care, Lydia Marmalade!' She burst into tears and ran out of the room.

Lydia was a little shocked, but moved that Martha had liked her, for she had – eventually – come to like Martha very much.

Her heart **thudded**. Surely after last night, after Lady Partridge being so warm to her, she wouldn't send Lydia away? But she *had* been found holding the stolen gems. Perhaps Lady Partridge refused to believe that Edmund had taken the necklace, so would blame Lydia anyway?

She got up and dressed quickly, going straight to the kitchen. If it was all over, she was going to take her Colin cuddles where she could get them; it didn't matter now that she behaved exactly as a *proper lady* should. She **bundled** him up in her arms and ran to the grand drawing room where she had come that first day.

Lady Partridge was at her desk, and she wasn't alone. On the chaise longue was Marianne, boots sodden with snow and eyes red as hawthorn berries. Next to her sat Edmund, his head bowed, looking more solemn than she'd ever seen him before.

'Ah, Lydia, please join us,' Lady Partridge said in a friendly tone, which Lydia thought was going to take some getting used to. 'You deserve an explanation.'

Lydia was caught off guard. She had been braced for being ordered to leave, but now what?

Edmund **cleared** his throat.

'Miss Marmalade, please accept our apologies.'

Marianne clearly couldn't bear it. 'Oh, Lydia! We are so sorry! None of this was your fault and we never wanted to embroil you in it!'

'It was I who took the necklace,' said Edmund. Lydia glanced at Lady Partridge, but she did not take her eyes off her son.

'He did it for me,' said Marianne. 'It was all a lie, you see. My family have no money at all. My father has lost it all in the city, in terrible investments, and my mother insisted the way to save us was for me to marry someone wealthy. The only thing we owned of worth was the necklace, an heirloom of my mother's.

I was to pretend to be wealthy to ensure a match with Edmund. But then the most unexpected thing happened – we truly fell in love, and I couldn't bear to lie to Edmund at all. So I told him the truth.'

They looked at each other with pure kindness.

'I wanted to help, fool that I am,' Edmund went on. 'We staged the theft so that I could sell the necklace privately, and at least give Marianne some money so that Mama would allow us to marry – but when I took it to a jeweller, he denounced it as a fake.'

'My father must have sold the original,' said Marianne. 'It was such a terrible thing that we did, and ever since we've been trying to fix the mess. Once we knew Lady Partridge believed Bertie and he was safe, we thought it might be forgotten. But then word reached our house this morning that Lydia had been accused, so I knew we had to confess.'

Lydia thought Ronalds must have been up at daybreak gossiping to anyone he could find, to start that rumour going so early. He really needed some hobbies in his life.

'Please, Mama, forgive us both.' Edmund hung his head in shame.

'I broke off the engagement because I did not want Edmund to marry me when he could marry someone so much better—'

'And I refused to let her marry anyone but me, for I love her!'

Lady Partridge **stared** at them both, her face clouded. Colin chose that moment to give an enormous **sneeze** accompanied by a rude sound from the other end, and for a moment Lydia thought Lady Partridge might be furious. But a smile spread across her face.

'What lucky children you are to find me today.' They all looked confused. 'It was not so long ago, I forgot that joy was not something that could be bought. In fact, I remembered only last night that it can never be purchased, but only fairly earned. *Happiness falls where it wants, no matter how fine your purse is*, as my dear cousin Catherine used to say.'

Lydia broke the silence. 'Does that … mean they can marry each other after all?'

Lady Partridge laughed. 'Yes, indeed! This marriage of love will make some others shake their heads and wonder if Edmund could have found a richer prospect, but I wholeheartedly approve of the match.'

Edmund and Marianne let out cries of happiness.

'Enough, enough fussing!' Lady Partridge adjusted the feathers in her hair.

'And Lydia,' Marianne held out her hand. 'You must be our bridesmaid, of course!'

'Oh, Marianne! Yes please!' They embraced like sisters.

Edmund **threw** his arms around Lady Partridge, who looked very flustered and very pleased.

Colin ran frantic circles around everyone, yapping

happily. 'Did you know, I had a dog once? When I was about Lydia's age.' Lady Partridge mused. 'A fine Pomeranian whom I named Cornelius, but whom Lydia's mother insisted on calling *Colin*, just like this reprobate. The most ridiculous name for a dog, of course, but we were both fond of the animal.'

Lydia sighed in satisfaction. That explained the dog collar!

She looked around at the drawing room: Christmas at Peppomberley wouldn't be the same as in Beech Cottage, in Hopperton, but Lydia thought she could bring the house some festive feeling. 'Shall we have carols around the piano tonight … Cousin Georgiana?'

'What an excellent idea,' Lady Partridge smiled. 'And maybe one of those most silly tunes your mother so loved, to bring in the Christmas spirit?'

Lydia **squeaked** with joy. And somewhere far away, she heard a ripple of bells.

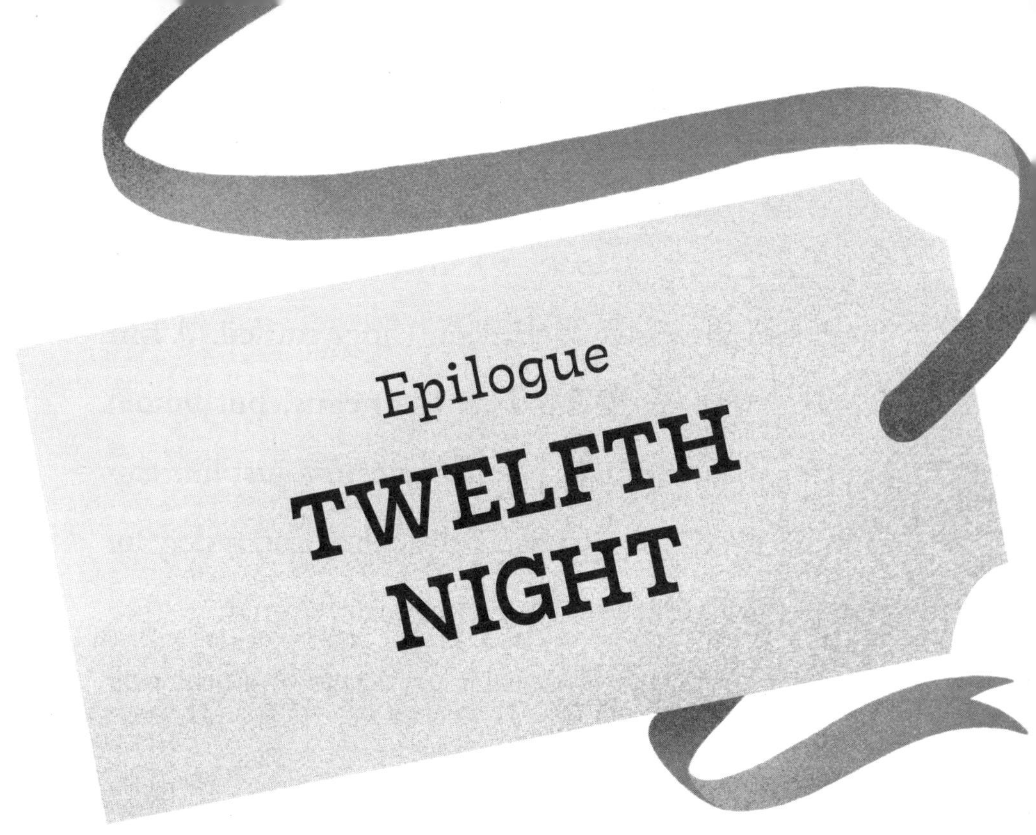

The bells of the church were ringing loudly as the snow fell upon the churchyard outside. They rang for the end of the winter season, Twelfth Night, the sixth of January, and also for Edmund and Marianne, newlywed and tumbling out of the church laughing with delight. Behind them came Lydia in a beautiful dress (borrowed from Marianne) holding a fresh sprig of holly, honeysuckle and mahonia, bound together with ivy, that Harriet had prepared fresh that morning.

Next came a happy-looking Lady Braun, telling all the guests how expensive her hat (and shoes, and shawl, and pelisse ...) was and behind her Lady Partridge, dressed head to toe in purple, her damson feathers bobbing as more snowflakes landed on them. Accompanying Lydia was Colin in a special green velvet bow that Harriet had made for him. He gave a *woof* of approval and then tried to run off to chase some robins.

Lady Partridge gave Lydia a small pat on the arm. It was slight but Lydia knew it meant a lot.

'It is a beautiful day for a wedding, is it not, Cousin Georgiana?'

'Indeed, Lydia, indeed.' Lydia moved away, just as Lady Braun sidled up to try and talk to Lady Partridge about all the Brauns moving into Peppomberley. Lady Partridge's eyebrows shot up in alarm and Lydia stifled a giggle.

Martha ran up to Lydia and gave her a quick hug, before racing back to Peppomberley to help prepare the wedding breakfast. Lydia had been practising and showed off her best curtsey yet to all the guests. She realised she felt truly happy. Colin was safe and loved his new home in the kitchen, Marianne was coming to live with them, and Bertie had been given a smart top hat and new shoes to drive the couple back home in the carriage. She stared at the sky, squinting in the bright snowfall. In the bare trees by the church gate, something caught her eye: a twinkling orange spark.

She **ran** towards it.

At the bottom of the lowest branch, swinging her legs, sat Bel, her skirt brightly aflame and her red hair **crackling** and **sparking**.

'Bel! You look so well!'

'Never felt better in my whole life, Lyddy-O!' She waved her star wand. Lydia looked down and saw snowdrops unfurling by her feet.

'Your magic! It works!'

'Oh, it feels good to have it back! Now I can turn that thieving Edmund into a fox-tailed frog. Where is he?'

'No! No, thank you, Bel. He's forgiven. We all are.' Lydia smiled. 'I'm so happy for you, Bel.'

'Me too, Miss Lyds. Stanley has done me a roast and all my pals are coming round to have a Twelfth Night party to celebrate the new year! Got two crates of acorn wine in and a load of Harriet's cakes too! She made mini ones for us. Couple of gluten-free ones for Stanley too, he gets terribly bloated otherwise.'

Bel's wings **unfurled** and Lydia saw they were a thousand shades of red and orange, glistening in the light. Another sprite in shades of ice blue called down to her from the top branches.

'All righ', keep your ears on, Meredith!' called Bel. 'She's moaning the potatoes will burn if we don't help Stanley out, he's rubbish with veg.'

She flew down and landed on Lydia's hand once more.

'Goodbye, Bel. And thank you – for everything.'

'Not goodbye, Miss Lyds. I'll see you when next season comes round, is what we sprites say.'

'See you when the next season comes round.'

Bel lifted her star wand one last time and waved it over Lydia. Her whole body filled with a **warm glow** that would stay with her for the rest of the month. Bel flew up to join the crowd of sprites that had gathered at the top of the oak tree. Lydia could see purple, pink, blue, yellow; a rainbow of sparkling magic that as quickly as it caught the light **disappeared** back into the forest.

Marianne appeared and threw her arms around Lydia's shoulders. 'My dearest sister Lydia!' she cried. 'You really are the slowest member of the Partridge family!'

The Partridge family. Lydia was part of a family again. She **closed** her eyes and felt the breeze on her face, her mother's voice speaking loud and clear. '*Whenever you need me, I am here.*' She knew this was what her mum had wanted – for Lydia to find a family again, to belong to people.

Back at Peppomberley, they would gather next to an enormous Christmas tree, a gift from Marianne's father to the family. The fires would be **blazing** against the cold outside, and all the rooms opened up and decorated with woodland greenery.

Ronalds, of course, would still be grumpy. He had lost his five-shilling wager to himself, and Lydia was still very much at Peppomberley. *Ah well,* thought Lydia. *You can't make everyone happy.*

'Come on, Lydia!' Marianne tugged at her sleeve. 'We need to get back to Peppomberley for the wedding breakfast, Harriet has made a nine-tiered sponge cake!'

Colin **yipped** at the word *cake*, and stopped work on the shrub he was trying to dig up, running as fast as his four short legs would carry him.

Bertie was preparing the horses, and he gave Lydia a wink. 'No stealing the horses now, Conker!'

Lydia **grinned**, and the whole village cheered and whooped as Edmund and Marianne got into the carriage.

Lydia rode with Lady Partridge and Lady Braun, Colin on her lap wound into a little bean shape. They turned out of the forest road and there it was,

Peppomberley, just as it had been that first day. This time, Lydia didn't see a giant, dark manor house; she saw lights, and rooms that she knew. She wasn't afraid. It wasn't what she had expected, but it was her **home**.

THE END

AUTHOR'S NOTE

Hello, I'm Cariad. I wrote this book, which is why I'm talking to you now. I wanted to write a very silly, funny, magical story that also talked about death.

When I was a teenager my dad died, and I felt very alone and as if no one really understood how I felt. If you read this book and you have a parent who has died as well, it might have brought up some big feelings for you. I just wanted to let you know that's OK. My dad died a very long time ago now – and some days I still feel sad about it and some days I feel OK. That's what grief is like – it comes and goes. As you get older it gets a little easier, but it can be very overwhelming at any age.

These days there are lots of brilliant charities for children who have experienced a loss. One of these I think is very helpful is Child Bereavement UK. You can have a look at their website to watch and read lots of information that might help you understand your grief or help someone who is going through a loss.

You can also always talk to a trusted adult. Even if you don't feel ready today, you can talk to them when you have the words or when you just need someone to sit with you.

Thank you for reading all about Lydia and Colin and their wish-tastrophe adventures.

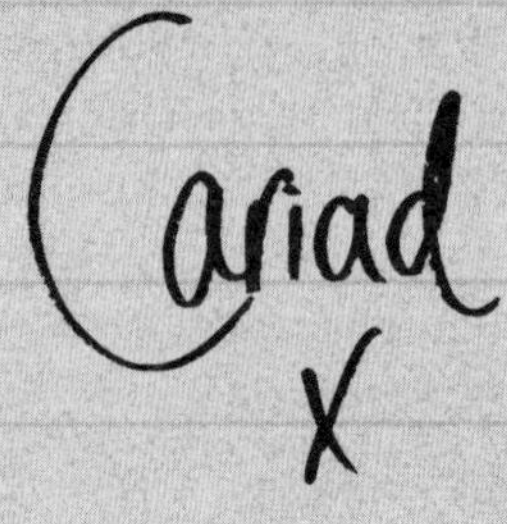

Child Bereavement UK helps children and young people (up to age 25) and their families to rebuild their lives when a child grieves or when a child dies.

Helpline: 0800 02 888 40

Live chat via the website

www.childbereavementuk.org

ALSO AVAILABLE AS AN AUDIO BOOK!

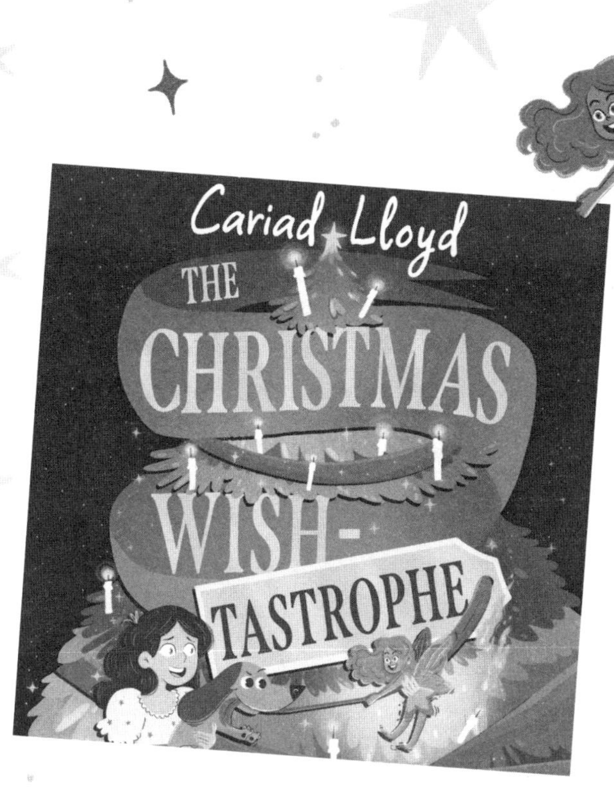

Photo © Yellowbelly Photos

Cariad Lloyd is a writer, actor, comedian, podcaster and improviser. She is the creator and host of the award-winning podcast *Griefcast* and author of the critically acclaimed *Times* bestseller *You Are Not Alone*, based on her grief lessons from the show.

Cariad has also appeared in *Peep Show*, *Alan Partridge*, *Have I Got News for You*, *QI* and a number of other comedy shows on TV and radio. She is one of the creators of hit improv show *Austentatious* and co-hosts *Sara and Cariad's Weirdos Book Club* podcast with Sara Pascoe.

X – **@LadyCariad** Instagram – **@cariadlloyd**